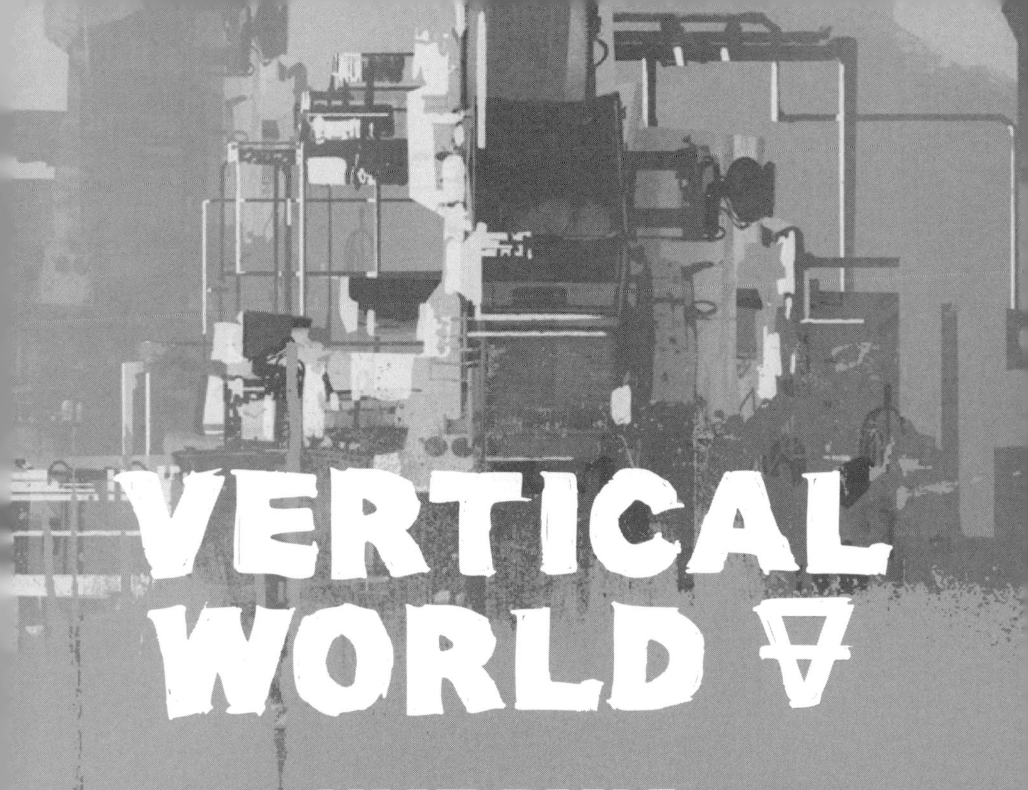

VERTICAL WORLD ∀

HYPOXIA

BY BRIAN CRAWFORD

EPIC Escape

An Imprint of EPIC Press
abdopublishing.com

Hypoxia

Vertical World: Book #4

abdopublishing.com

Published by EPIC Press, a division of ABDO, PO Box 398166, Minneapolis, Minnesota 55439. Copyright © 2019 by Abdo Consulting Group, Inc. International copyrights reserved in all countries. No part of this book may be reproduced in any form without written permission from the publisher. Escape™ is a trademark and logo of EPIC Press.

Printed in the United States of America, North Mankato, Minnesota.
052018
092018

♻

Cover design by Christina Doffing
Images for cover art obtained from iStockphoto.com
Edited by Gil Conrad

Library of Congress Cataloging-in-Publication Data

Library of Congress Control Number: 2018932904

Publisher's Cataloging in Publication Data

Names: Crawford, Brian, author.
Title: Hypoxia/ by Brian Crawford
Description: Minneapolis, MN : EPIC Press, 2019 | Series: Vertical world; #4
Summary: Having survived a firefight with Cthonians below, Rex and Aral flee back up to Ætheria. As soon as they arrive, the two are separated and interrogated. Facing his government's refusal to accept the truth about Cthonia, Rex embarks on a quest to find Aral and rescue her from torture and imprisonment by the ever-more-paranoid Head Ductor, the ruler of Ætheria.
Identifiers: ISBN 9781680769142 (lib. bdg.) | ISBN 9781680769425 (ebook)
Subjects: LCSH: Massacre survivors--Fiction. | Survival--Fiction--Fiction. | Revolutions--Fiction--Fiction. | Science fiction--Societies, etc--Fiction | Young adult fiction.
Classification: DDC [FIC]--dc23

This series is dedicated to Debbie Pearson.
Thank you for everything.

ONE

EVERYONE KNEW THERE WERE NO MISSTEPS IN Ætheria.

Everyone knew that making a simple mistake could get you Tossed—thrown off of the edge of Tátea to plummet thirty thousand feet to your death. It had happened before.

But until sixteen-year-old Rex Himmel emerged from *below* with the Cthonian girl, no one had ever heard of the Ætherian Council using torture to get answers.

Ætheria's parts warehouse and descent pod hangar were in tumult. No sooner had Rex and Aral emerged from Unit Alif's fatal mission to Cthonia than dozens of ACF hands grasped at both of them, scooping them out of their cramped, shared pod. Pushing through the others, Deputy Head Schlott—leader of the Ætherian Cover Force—grabbed Rex and pulled him off to the side, bombarding him with concerned questions that, to Rex, seemed lightning fast: "Are you okay? How do you feel? The five others made it up. Where's the rest of your team? Where's Yoné? What happened? You're going to be a hero. You need rest . . ."

But while she comforted him, a different scene was unfolding back at the open pod—a scene hidden from Rex's view. Working under direct orders from Schlott given seconds before she pulled Rex away, seven or eight ACF scouts had swooped onto Aral, binding her feet, hands, eyes, and mouth, and yanking her writhing body from the descent pod. Already weakened by the thin air at this altitude, Aral groaned through her gag and struggled against her captors. But it was no use—even though she was physically much larger than the Ætherians, she couldn't fight off all of them. Even if she had been able to resist, they were all armed with Stær guns. And just one shot from these weapons would instantly incapacitate her with one hundred thousand volts. What would happen if she received seven or eight charges at once? No one—not even a gigantic Cthonian—could withstand such a surge of electricity. She didn't know any of this right then, but her only option was to let herself be carried off.

"Aral?!" Rex asked, turning toward the chaos that echoed through the warehouse. As soon as he rotated to try and find the Cthonian who'd helped them below, Schlott brusquely turned him around and directed him toward the metal door leading outside. Rex hadn't heard her bark "Capture the infiltrator!" as soon as Aral had sat up in the pod. All he'd heard was Schlott's barrage of questions and the sound of the ACF rushing in as the pod hatch opened.

Steering him away from the pods, Deputy Head Schlott wound Rex through awkwardly stacked metal barrels, tapping his shoulder as she spoke, but never really releasing her grip.

"Don't worry about her . . . about that . . . *Cthonian*. We need to get you to a doctor—get you checked out. You've been through a lot."

———

Unbeknownst to Rex, both he and Aral arrived at Ætheria's Sanatorium Complex one island away at the same time—he through the front; Aral through the back. But while he was directed to a sterile room for a medical examination, Aral was strapped down to a bed while seven ACF Protectors hovered over her. Already weak from hypoxia at this high altitude and drifting in and out of consciousness, she did not resist. They removed her blindfold and gag, leaving her gasping like a fish out of water.

Among her guards were Protectors Challies and Roman. Within minutes, Ætheria's Head Ductor himself showed up. Prior to Rex and Aral's arrival in

Ætheria, he'd already been alerted to the discovery of the Cthonian by the five scouts from Unit Alif who'd come back up just as Yoné, Rex, and the others had left for the Cthonian Cave Complex down below. As the only members of the Ætherian High Command present, only Roman and the Head Ductor wore personal oxygen tanks, which clicked and hissed as they breathed. When the group had barged into the medical room, they had locked the door behind them, preventing any of the Sanatorium staff from entering.

"Air . . . " Aral muttered in a weak, almost inaudible voice as her arms were fastened down. Her eyes fixed onto the Protectors' oxygen canisters, then they rolled back in her head. She tried to focus on her captors, but could not hold their gaze. "Please. I can't breathe. Help . . . " She squinted, holding back tears. A thunderous headache racked her temples—one of the first signs of hypoxia, the deadly altitude sickness.

"What's that?" the Head Ductor said in a squeaky, almost mouse-like voice. His words came in clipped bursts, as if he were holding in a violent temper that could explode at any second. "The Cthonian *can* talk? What did she say?" His oxygen tank hissed along with his words.

"She can't breathe," Challies said, his eyes shifting back and forth between Aral and the HD. Like the others in the room, his body tingled with a nervous energy. *Why had she come up with Rex? What could she tell them about the Cthonians' motives?*

"So," the HD said. Stepping up to the bed, he wiped back his greasy black hair over a balding head. "You want air? Air?! First *you* help us, then we help you."

As their leader spoke, the other ACF scouts stood rapt. They knew he was not to be toyed with. They felt his anger. They also sensed his fear. Ætheria was under attack, and here was perhaps the only person—this Cthonian—who could help them understand why.

"Wake up!" he suddenly shouted, making the others jump. He rapped Aral in the shoulder—not hard enough to cause pain, but hard enough to jolt her from her fading consciousness. She opened her eyes and searched the room for his voice. But her eyes were cloudy, unfocused.

"Wha . . . ?" she slurred.

"What happened to the rest of our team? Twelve Ætherians went down. Six came up—and one with you. This . . . it was Rex Himmel, right?" He glanced around the room and then back at her. "Where are the others? The ones who didn't come up? Our pods detected that they were killed. Who are you? Are *you* responsible for their deaths? Talk!"

When Aral didn't answer, he looked up to Roman and snapped, "Get her air. She has to talk." His temples glistened with sweat.

Roman rushed from the room and returned seconds later with a Sanatorium nurse, who wheeled in a large oxygen tank and installed it next to Aral's bed. The employee worked quickly, keeping his eyes averted from the Head Ductor's. It was only too clear to him what the HD's intentions were, but he also knew what he risked if he did not immediately comply.

There are no missteps in Ætheria.

"Get it on her," the HD yipped. As the nurse worked, the Head Ductor clasped both hands over his nose and mouth and sucked desperately at his oxygen supply tube. His tank hissed and spat as if he were trying to drain it in one breath. The other scouts threw a glance at him but quickly looked back to the prisoner.

The nurse fumbled with the tank's valve, twisting it hard clockwise. At the same time, he unhooked a coiled length of transparent plastic tubing attached to the tank's nozzle. With a loud *hisssss*, a burst of air flowed through the tube, causing the end to flap about under the pressure of the escaping air. He stepped over to Aral and worked the nosepiece into her nostrils and the ends of the tube around her ears to hold the apparatus in place. She recoiled at his touch, but her head lolled to the side. She squeezed her eyes shut at the sudden pressure of the air inside her nose. Though she didn't speak or open her eyes, her facial muscles relaxed and she breathed deeply, as if she understood what was happening.

"Leave," the HD said to the nurse after Aral had taken several breaths. The nurse bowed his head and shuffled out, closing the door gently behind him. The HD lowered his hands from his face and panted like someone who'd just run a race.

Over the next few minutes, the ACF Protectors and the HD stood like angry statues over their prisoner. As she took breath after breath of pure oxygen, color quickly returned to her otherwise pale features. Several minutes passed, with the only sound being that of the three whistling oxygen canisters in the room: the HD's, Roman's, and Aral's. As for Challies, he kept his eyes on the Cthonian as she stirred back to life. Despite his apprehension, part of him struggled with the unfairness of the scene—not for Aral's sake, but for him and the other ACF. He knew the rules. He knew the ranks. But couldn't shake the burning desire to wear his own oxygen mask. Still, would she talk now?

"Can you hear me?" the HD said as Aral stirred.

She slowly opened her eyes. They lolled around the room before settling on the Head Ductor. She nodded.

"Good. Can you understand me?"

Nod.

"Do you know where you are?"

"Yes." Aral's voice was weak.

"Okay. We have some questions." The HD wrung his hands as he spoke. His voice seemed calmer than before. "Answer truthfully and nothing will happen. Hesitate and," he looked up at Roman and nodded, "we will turn off your oxygen. Do you know what hypoxia is?"

Aral shook her head no.

"It's when your body shuts down because it can't breathe." The HD leaned in close. "First you get headaches. Then vomiting, delirium, wheezing . . . and you know what happens then, if you don't get oxygen right away?"

"You . . . " Aral began.

"You die a painful death as your brain swells inside your skull."

The HD stood up straight and folded his arms. His oxygen canister hissed and clicked as he breathed. He stared at the Cthonian and said nothing, letting his words sink in. He finally turned to Roman and nodded, shifting his eyes to Aral's tank. He looked back at the prisoner.

"So why did you attack us?" he asked. "Are there any more attacks planned?"

Aral's eyes widened and she shook her head. "No, wait, it was a mistake. We didn't attack. It was . . . "

But the Head Ductor cut her off. "Turn her oxygen off," he snapped at Roman.

Challies winced at what he was witnessing. His urge was to stop Roman, but he restrained himself, knowing what would happen if he defied the HD.

Without hesitating, Roman twisted the tank's valve counterclockwise.

"No lies," the HD said in a chilling voice. "Tell me what I want to hear, or you will die."

Aral's screams echoed through the halls of the Sanatorium. But as the oxygen left her body, her screams quickly died to a whimper.

Followed by silence.

TWO

REX WOKE UP.

Before he opened his eyes, he heard noises. Beeping. Hissing. Clicking. Rhythmic tapping. The sounds came from his left, a few feet from his shoulder.

Rex lay on his back on a bed or cot. He couldn't tell where he was, but it was soft. He stretched his legs and arms, which felt stiff and sore. His muscles ached. His joints creaked. Even his fingers moved slowly, lethargically. He felt as though a weight were sitting on his chest, keeping him from filling his lungs. Something was wrong. He wasn't getting enough air.

He reached his hands up to rub his eyes, which had become crusted over with sleep. Something pulled at his left forearm, keeping him from bending it upward. With his right hand free, he fingered his eyes open and blinked. A piercing white light stung his retinas. He squeezed his eyes shut as they adjusted. Tears formed under his eyelids. He opened them again, blinking slowly. He lifted his head and looked around.

Rex was in a clinic room. He was alone. It was a small chamber, about seven by ten feet—just big enough for his folding medical bed to fit and give doctors or whomever room to walk around to inspect him. The walls were white and bare, but the ceiling was composed solely of glaring lights. It was as if the entire room was designed as some sort of massive microscope with him as a specimen under the glowing lens. Several feet from the left foot of his bed, a shiny metallic door sealed him in from the rest of Ætheria.

He had no memory of being brought here.

He turned to the left and saw a stack of machines

that beeped and hissed and whirred. Red LED numbers flashed on a small screen:

```
HR 83 O2 84 BP 162/64 TEMP 95.6 SC 13%.
```

These were his vitals. He glanced at his left forearm. A needle plunged into his artery, a clear liquid trickling into his veins from an IV bag held a few feet above the bed by a metal rack. The needle had been taped to his skin with translucent surgical tape. As he moved to look at the machines, Rex felt another tug from under his shirt. He looked down and realized two things: he was dressed in a light blue-and-pink clinic gown, and four or five small black wires wound their way under the cloth, where they were attached to his chest with sticky sensor pads.

Something dug into his right wrist. The Tracker was still attached. Of course. The very thought that the Ætherian Council was watching his every move with this crude, plastic-and-metal device made his temples throb with frustration. Why was it that every member of the ACF had to wear one of these? As if they were all criminals that had to be watched and listened to. Was the Ætherian Council really that worried?

Even though he'd only moved a few inches, Rex's head spun from the effort. He flopped back down onto his pillow.

Rex closed his eyes and tried to remember what had gotten him here. He found thinking difficult, as his head pounded with each heartbeat. He was unable to form coherent thoughts. Only disconnected images danced behind his closed eyelids: the explosion that caused Ætheria's Power Works on Tátea to fall; climbing down the Proboscis tube to search for Cthonian spies; training with the other Ætherian Cover Force scouts; going down to Cthonia in the descent pod; the acid rain; the burning rubble; the Cthonian airship shooting at them; Yoné and the team getting shot; and Aral, the Cthonian . . .

Aral, whom Rex had never met before, but who recognized him as Máire Himmel's son. Máire Himmel, who'd been living among the Cthonians for sixteen years—precisely the amount of time since Rex's mom had left him as a newborn. Upon their first meeting, Aral had recognized his name, she had recognized his half-paralyzed face, and she had even confirmed that the woman in Rex's small photograph was indeed his mother. Apparently anyone in Cthonia who knew Máire also knew of her son, who she talked about with anyone who'd listen . . .

Rex sat up.

"Mom!" he said aloud, turning his head in a growing panic. "Aral . . . "

Despite his aching muscles and throbbing head, Rex turned to his left and looked at the machines. They sat there stoically, stupidly, beeping away to themselves as they monitored his vital signs. Then he saw it. Just above the top machine, a red button was affixed in the center of a three-by-four-inch silver wall plate. A small label with the words Nurse Call was affixed just above the plate.

With a pained groan, Rex leaned his body over to his right and pushed the button. It lit up and blinked steadily, one blink per second. Rather than lie back down, Rex pulled his pillow up against the wall lengthwise, so that he could inch backwards and lean his back against the wall. Now seated, he glanced back at the machines.

HR 123 O2 83 BP 168/66 TEMP 96.2 SC 13%

The light continued to blink.

Within a minute or so, a metallic clicking and rustling clattered at the door. Rex was surprised. He hadn't heard any footsteps outside. The door opened slowly and calmly. A man in his early thirties stepped in. Though his skin was smooth and youthful, his hair was prematurely gray and slicked back against his scalp. He wore greenish scrubs and a small, index card-sized ID badge swung from a lanyard around his neck. Seeing the nurse's clothing, Rex realized neither he nor the nurse were wearing their AeroGel suits—the highly insulated outfits that all Ætherians wore to protect them from the constant, subfreezing, stratospheric temperatures of the Ætherian floating islands.

The clinic was heated. It must've been hooked up to a generator. Because in the attack on Tátea's Power Works four days earlier, all power and water had been cut from Ætheria. Only those few buildings with generators and water reserves could expect to maintain life—just long enough for the ACF to repair the Proboscis, which drew water and highly flammable cthoneum gas from the Cthonian earth six miles below.

"Yes?" the nurse said, stepping into the room and sidling up to Rex. The nurse's eyes danced over Rex's IV connection and the machines. He was clearly running through a mental checklist to make sure Rex's vitals were being monitored and his IV was still fully connected, the bag was full of fluid, and the connection was still unobstructed. Rex noticed the nurse never made eye contact.

"What's going on?" Rex asked. "Why am I here?"

The nurse stepped back and looked Rex in the eye.

His expression went blank. He seemed to be thinking whether he should say anything.

"Hmm," was all he could muster. He turned and walked out of the room, closing the door behind him with a click.

Rex felt his anger and frustration growing, as well as fear. Why did the nurse ignore him? Why was he being held here? He didn't have any medical problems. In fact, he had just descended into Cthonia and reascended with nothing going wrong. On the contrary, the air down below had been almost like a drug, making him feel stronger and healthier than he ever had before.

He lunged over again and pressed the Nurse Call button, which had stopped blinking when the nurse had opened the door. The blinking resumed.

This time, several minutes passed before anyone arrived. Trying to calm himself, Rex lay back and closed his eyes. He listened to his rhythmic breathing and focused on the coursing red of his eyelids, which were lit mercilessly from above.

The door clicked and opened.

Rex jumped back up.

"Well?" he said, before registering who had opened the door.

"Yes?" a woman's voice answered from behind the swiveling door. Rex shifted his eyes.

This time, what looked to be a doctor strode in, followed by the mute nurse from before. The woman looked surprisingly young for a doctor—maybe in her mid-twenties—but Rex reasoned that she must've just looked young. Her eyes were a piercing blue. As she studied Rex, she seemed not to blink. She took in everything, like some sort of hawk or spy.

"Rex?" she said, now fully in the room. "Rex Himmel?" The mute stood behind her and shifted his eyes back and forth between the back of her head and Rex. But the nurse never made eye contact with him. His eyes were shifty. If the doctor reminded Rex of a raptor, the nurse reminded him of a weasel.

"Yes?"

"How are you feeling?"

"I'm fine. Of course," Rex blinked and shook his head, "I've got a headache."

"That's not surprising. Your body has gone through a lot since yesterday. I'm Doctor Repal. I've been put in charge of monitoring you until you are better."

"What do you mean? Better? I'm fine! Even down there, down in Cthonia, I mean, I didn't even get hurt or . . . " he paused, his thoughts drifting to Yoné and his other teammates, who'd died down below, shot by the Cthonian aircraft.

"Well, no, you don't have any injuries. But your oxygen saturation levels have been fluctuating wildly. We've never seen levels all over the charts like yours. We can only conclude that the toxic air from your time in Cthonia has caused your lungs to—"

"There *is* no toxic air," Rex snapped, looking up. "My mask came off down there. Didn't anyone tell you that? And the air is fine. I could breathe! We all could breathe! Every single one of us pulled off our masks and *nothing happened.* I'm telling you, it's much better than the air up here. Like there was more oxygen in it or something. It was like when they gave us the oxygen tanks, only without any masks . . . "

Dr. Repal paused. She looked embarrassed—not for herself, but for Rex. As if he'd just made a fool of himself and she was letting him recover.

"Where's Aral?" he asked.

"What?"

"Aral. The girl. The tall girl from Cthonia. She came up with me. She was helping us."

"I don't know what you mean. You are the only one who was brought to us. You have been here for about seven hours." There was something forced, artificial, about the tone in her voice. Rex had the distinct impression Repal was lying. His anger grew.

"But I—I mean, we—I came up with a Cthonian. She's on our side, and she might know my . . . " he hesitated before continuing. "Look, I'm telling you!" Rex felt a pinch in his arm, as if the IV needle were digging farther into his artery. "You're saying I've been here—asleep—since I came up?"

"I understand that you're upset," Repal continued, her voice steady and unwavering. "But you were the only patient submitted to us for treatment for pulmonary toxicity. You've breathed in too much poison, and it takes a while to filter that out of . . . "

"That air down there is *not* poison!" Rex shouted, sitting up tall. His heart pounded in his ears. "I could breathe just fine! And now you're telling me that someone is missing who clearly helped us down there? Her name is Aral. She has long, black hair, and is about a foot taller than anyone up here. And she's pale—much paler than we are. Her name is Aral! Aral!"

Repal didn't answer. Her face kept a neutral expression. She breathed calmly, but kept her eyes on Rex. Only when Rex's breathing slowed did she shift her gaze from him to the machines to his left. Rex watched her black pupils dance over the displays.

"Your oxygen saturation has returned to a normal level. Eighty-seven percent. Your blood and system are stabilizing to altitude. You are no longer at risk for hypoxia. You were lucky."

Rex averted his eyes and bit down on his lower lip. He was clearly going to get nowhere with her. Repal took a deep breath and folded her arms.

"We can probably take you off of fluids and the drip. We should be able to get you back into your normal AG suit. First, though, there's someone who wants to talk to you."

THREE

"**D**EPUTY HEAD SCHLOTT?"

"Rex. Good to see you better. Have a seat." Schlott's oxygen tank hissed as she spoke.

Rex sat in the soft blue seat opposite Schlott's desk. The two were in Schlott's small office, located in Bernuac HQ. Behind Schlott three ACF Protectors stood, their hands behind their backs. Each wore the standard-issue ACF uniform, their badges shining dimly in the center of their chests. One of the men was Protector Challies, the Protector who'd first been assigned to Rex's case. The two made eye contact, and Rex thought he saw the hint of a smile. Challies averted his eyes to Schlott. None of the three were wearing supplemental oxygen.

Rex shifted in his seat. He couldn't help letting his eyes fall on the small tube leading from Schlott's nostrils to an oxygen container hidden behind her. There those tanks were, again. *If only they knew about the air down in Cthonia,* he thought.

At the thought, Rex squirmed uncomfortably. Before leaving the clinic, he'd been given a new AG suit to wear. The suit squeezed his torso and rubbed against his sore arm and chest, where six adhesive sensors had been glued since he'd been admitted last night. The walk over had been labored. Even though he'd spent barely a full day in the oxygen-rich Cthonian atmosphere, his body struggled to readjust to the rarefied air of Ætheria. He'd spent his entire life at thirty thousand feet, but it felt as if his brief time in the thicker, more life-giving air down below had wiped out his body's memory of how to survive at this altitude. His feet felt heavy and cumbersome. His head ached. He felt nauseous. Spots danced in front of his eyes. To get here from the Sanatorium Complex, he had to cross two Zipp lines. At first he'd been nervous he would incorrectly attach his harness and fall to his death. Before crossing, he'd checked the carabiners five times. Only then did he push off and cross the expanse, the Zipp line's metal pulley buzzing just over his head. The churning Welcans cloud boiled two thousand feet below his dangling legs.

"How are you feeling?" Schlott asked. Her mute companions remained stone-faced.

"I'm getting there. But this headache won't leave."

"I understand. It's probably low-grade altitude sickness. Though that should pass. You've been through a lot."

Rex nodded and lowered his eyes. *Would they stop saying that?*

"Until permanent arrangements can be made, you'll have a home here with the ACF. Food. Lodging. Education. Training. We'll look after you. But more on that later," Schlott continued. "Right now, um, well, first I guess I should congratulate you on your work." Schlott leaned over her desk and fumbled through a stack of papers. "Really heroic, actually. Who knows? Maybe you'll get a plaque, an award, something. You are part of history, you know?"

Rex nodded dumbly. He reached his left hand over and rubbed his right wrist, where the Tracker continued to dig into his skin.

"Deputy Head Schlott?"

"Yes?"

"Is there any chance you could take this off now? You know I'm not going to . . . "

"I see, I see," Schlott interrupted, letting her eyes fall on the device. "I understand, but, um . . . "

"Yes?"

"Well, it's just that we're bound by procedure. All ACF and Ætherian Council members wear them. Even me, see?" Schlott lifted her left arm and pulled the sleeve of her AG suit back to reveal a Tracker identical to his.

Rex nodded but avoided Schlott's eyes.

"What about an oxygen tank, like you? Like everyone in the High Command. Is that possible?"

"Hmm." Schlott looked over her shoulder at the men behind her. "I'll pass on a recommendation. We'll see. Maybe . . . After all, who can deny that what you did requires a lot of guts—guts and sacrifice. Going down there into a toxic environment . . . perhaps you deserve a promotion. And that could at least get you closer to having one."

Rex jerked his head up and watched Schlott intently. Schlott didn't notice. Her eyes continued to scan the papers on her desk as she read aloud.

" . . . coming under fire, escaping, being the only one of the team to make it up. That is, other than the five others who came up before you. Your work will be helpful. Given what you say about the hostile forces down there, it makes things too risky for us to send anyone else down. If we were to send people down into that armed group that attacked you, they'd be sitting ducks. No, too dangerous." Schlott paused, lost in thought. "Let's just hope there's no other attack."

"Deputy Head?"

"Yes?" Schlott looked up, but the fingers of her left hand slid over the top few sheets.

"You said, 'one'?"

"Sorry?"

Rex sat up straight. "You said only one of us came back up. Me."

"Yes, that's right."

"There were two of us. You were there. You saw her."

"Excuse me?"

"*Two* of us came up, not one. Aral, and me. Aral, the Cthonian. Surely, the five others told you as well. They saw her before coming back. Where is she? She's the one who . . ."

Schlott put up her hand, cutting Rex off. She closed her eyes and shook her head. The men behind her exchanged glances. Only Protector Challies seemed lost in his own thoughts.

"Son, you've gone through a lot. I'm sure by now your head is . . . "

"*And* I could breathe just fine down there. Didn't they tell you? Where are they?" Rex looked around, as if expecting to see the five other scouts there in the office with them. He turned back to Schlott and continued, his words coming faster and faster. "It's hard to believe, I know, but the air is just fine to breathe. Things must've changed since Ætheria was founded, I'm telling you. How long ago was that, almost a thousand years? My mask came off, and—"

"Rex," Schlott interrupted. She sighed and took a deep breath, her eyes intent on Rex's. She sat back and folded the fingers of her two hands together. Unblinking, she stared deep into Rex's eyes. Rex held her gaze. Schlott looked down and slid some sheets of paper from a closed folder. Rex glanced at the papers. The top few appeared to be some type of forms. The other papers were blank.

"Rex," Schlott repeated. "I hear what you are saying. But right now . . . now that you've been released from care and you're awake, up and about . . . " She turned slightly and glanced over her left shoulder.

Challies looked at Schlott and nodded slightly, almost imperceptibly. "Don't worry about the others. They've been taken care of. All you need to do is this: we need a report from you." Schlott slid the forms over. Rex leaned forward and pulled them into his lap. As Rex thumbed through the pages, Schlott continued.

"We've already recovered your communication recording and retrieved your vital stats from the descent pod. But what we *don't* have is your take on things. Eyewitness report, I guess you could call it. So there." She nodded. "You need to fill those out for us, and then on the blank paper, it would be most helpful if you could draw a map of what you saw in as much detail as you can, along with approximate distances, topography, and so on. All in relation to your landing site, of course. This will also be a good place for you to tell us about . . . what did you say her name was . . . Aral?"

"Yes, that's right." Rex felt a slight wave of relief that he would be able to explain everything as it actually happened. "Deputy Head?"

"Yes?"

"Could I see my vital stats? I mean, could I see the record of my stats while I was down there?"

Two of the men squirmed. Challies shot Rex a look. Schlott wrinkled her nose.

"Why do you want that? They're normal, so you shouldn't have anything to worry about."

Rex nodded. "Okay, so . . . can I see them? I told you: my mask came off, and for half the time I was breathing fine—better than fine, really. I don't know how to say it, but the air down there made me fe stronger. I was wondering if there was any difference in my oxygen saturation—I don't know, a spike or something? You know, when I started breathing the denser air, did my O2 levels . . . "

"I told you," Schlott interrupted. "Your. Stats.

Were. Normal. That's what happened. And that's the version that's been submitted to Ætheria's ComCenter. It is out of your hands. And mine. Just put your story down there, as best as you can recall."

A silence fell over the room.

"Okay . . . " Rex mumbled. "I'll . . . I'll do these, then." He felt his face burn as he turned to the papers.

He suddenly wanted to be out of there—away from Schlott and the others. What was Schlott hiding . . . beyond the fact that she seemed to be denying Aral's existence? What did Schlott know that Rex didn't? Why did nobody seem to be interested in hearing about the air down below? Why did it seem like they wanted a story that wasn't true? Unless, maybe his brain was playing tricks on him? Maybe Rex hadn't thought everything through and really was jumping to brash conclusions? But at the thought of Aral—Aral, who'd clearly stated she knew his mother—a panicked worry flashed through his mind. What if Aral was dead? What if she'd been locked up? Or worse? Rex needed Aral right now more than anyone else. Given Schlott's reaction when he asked about Aral, Rex thought it best he not even mention his mother. Now only Aral could help him solve this puzzle that had been hovering in his mind his entire life . . .

Rex picked up the pen Schlott slid over and began filling out the top form. As he wrote in his last name, first name, middle initial(s), ACF identification number, he scoured his memory for any trace of having heard about a prison on Ætheria. Aside from the interrogation room on Tátea where he'd been brought after Challies and Roman forced him to enlist in the ACF a week before, he knew of none. While he'd been alive, his foster dad had never mentioned any prisons. And he would've known, being the Ætherian Council's head of Energy and Survival. No, the only punishment his foster dad had ever mentioned was the Tossings—when criminals were thrown from the edge of one of the islands to plunge to their deaths below.

Rex lowered the pen to the top sheet.

ACF Incident and Reconnaissance Form

Section 1: Last Name: Himmel

Section 1A: First Name: Rex

Section 1B: Middle Initial: S.

Section 1C: ACF Identification Number: 1421

Section 1D: Height: 5'9"

Section 1E: Weight: 165

Section 1F: Date of Birth:

Section 2: Date of Mission:

Section 2A: Objective:

Section 2B: Team Members Present:

Section 2C: Equipment:

Section 3: Standard Procedure and ACF Protocols:

Section 4: Narration of Mission:

Under the eyes of the three ACF Protectors and Schlott, Rex scratched in his answers, the sound of the pen adding a grating *scritchscritchscritch* to the buzzing in his ears. Twenty minutes passed. When he reached section 37B: `Unusual, aberrant, or unplanned events not prescribed by protocol`, Rex lifted the pen and looked up.

"What do you want . . . um, what should I write here?" Rex pointed at the prompt with the pen's cap end.

"Which one?" Schlott sat up straight and peered over her desk. She raised her eyebrows but squinted.

"Number 37, part B. What does it mean by 'unusual'?"

"Oh." Schlott relaxed her back. "Just anything unplanned . . . any surprises."

"Should I put the part about my mask coming off?"

"No." Schlott shook her head slightly. "Just stick to what happened."

Rex was starting to get the point. Nothing happened down there. No Aral. No clean air. He felt a twinge of fear mixed with anger—as if pushing the truth on these four would put him in danger. He leaned his back against the chair and scanned Schlott's face. He was being asked to lie . . . on an official form.

"Under 37B, you should make sure to put the details of your Point's murder," Schlott added. "The ACC will want *those* details."

"The Ætherian Central Command?"

"Yes."

"Hmm."

Rex wrote:

After we had left the area of the crash, we were going to sleep for the night. Before that, we sent back five scouts to inform Ætherian High Command that we'd found a live Cthonian. Then a Cthonian airship arrived. It had several lights and was scanning the ground. Aral said that whoever was in the plane was probably looking for us. She said whoever was in the plane had been sent to investigate where the Proboscis had fallen. She'd said that her people were running out of water, and that's what had led them to us.

The plane flew by us but didn't stop. It was only a little bit after it had passed overhead that it turned around and circled back. The plane hovered for a while. But my Stær gun misfired in the direction of the airship. It was an accident. The pilots immediately started shooting. We fled on four-legged animals the Cthonians called eqūs, animals that can run much faster than a person. The plane followed and kept shooting.

That was when Yoné was shot, along with the rest of the team. We couldn't stop to get any of the bodies. We had to get to the pods and back up to Ætheria. Aral and I were the only ones to make it back up. All of the other descent pods had already been sent up to transmit the alarm. So we had to share.

When Rex had finished, he clutched the pen, which had become slippery under his sweat. With his right hand, he massaged his left, which ached from the writing. Schlott leaned over and pulled the completed form across the desk.

Over the next few minutes, Schlott read silently, the three other men peering over her shoulder as she did. Her eyes darted over Rex's words. She worked her jaw muscles as she read, focused and intent.

When Schlott had finished, the Deputy Head eased her right hand over to a pen holder and removed a black marker, which she uncapped. Without saying anything to Rex, Schlott brought the marker to Rex's report and blacked out several lines of his text, the felt tip squeaking across the paper as she moved her hand from left to right. Rex inched his head upward to cast a glance on what Schlott was removing.

She was deleting every sentence where Rex

mentioned Aral. Rex's face went cold and a nauseous cramp gripped his stomach.

FOUR

"WHERE ARE WE GOING?" REX ASKED THE three ACF Protectors who walked him out of Schlott's office. Two of the men stepped on either side of him and Challies, behind him. Prior to today, Rex had never seen the other two men before. Only Challies's eyes held a hint of humanity.

"Bernuac HQ," Challies said in a raspy voice. "Just one Zipp away. Let's move."

Thirty minutes later, the four stepped into the ACF Training Facility at Bernuac HQ. Rex walked through the hatch, and the three men followed. The sudden warmth from the heated building made Rex feel as if his muscles were melting. He shook his hands to chase away the cold as the four walked down a short hall and turned left. When they walked through the hatch leading into the main training room, a surprise greeted Rex.

When he had been here a week ago, Rex had seen a completely bare room—almost like a gym with a white, shiny floor. It had been here that the different units of scouts had assembled before their first descent into the Proboscis. It was here that Rex had met Yoné, his Point and mentor who'd taken him under her wing before leading Rex down to Cthonia.

Now, both Yoné and Unit Alif were dead. And the five others? Where were they? What had Schlott meant by "They've been taken care of"? He looked around the room, but saw them nowhere. Strange. Surely they'd be involved in any work the ACF was involved in?

The room was filled with tables and dozens of people—not just uniformed members of the ACF, but regular Ætherians as well. And all were working together.

There must've been at least fifty tables, each four by eight feet long. They were arranged in rows, with space in between for several people to walk. The ACF and the regular Ætherians buzzed about in activity. Some were seated at the tables. Some stood. Some walked back and forth, shuffling around stacks of paper on the tables. From his place in the hatch, Rex couldn't tell what they were working on. He could see that images and text were printed on the papers, but he couldn't see what the text said or what the images showed. At the head of each table, someone sat typing into a NotaScript. Each of the typists were intent on what they were doing. They looked up only now and then to say something to one or more of the people working at their tables.

"Since the attack, we've had hundreds of people turn up to help: ACF or not," Challies said. "There's so much to do. Everyone wants to help: rebuild the Proboscis, maintain the remaining water and electricity, ration the food, and whatnot. It seems like everyone on Ætheria wants to help, and we've accepted quite a few volunteers. This way," he said, placing his palm on Rex's left elbow. The four walked forward, but the room was so crowded, Rex had to shift his torso left and right to avoid bumping into people who were buried in their work and oblivious to his presence. Some carried stacks of paper so thick that it seemed that at any moment, they would drop their loads, sending papers scattering across the floor.

"There," Challies said after they had worked their way to the far corner of the room. Rex followed the Protector's gaze to one of the tables that still had some space. There, an ACF scout was working with her head down, scanning a pile of printed documents spread out in front of her.

"This is Ama, one of our top scouts," Challies said. Ama looked up—first at Challies and then at Rex. She stood and held out her hand. The other two ACF Protectors watched intently.

"Are you Rex?"

"Yes . . . " Rex muttered, taken aback by yet another person who knew who he was.

"Ama, Rex has been posted here on your team," Challies said. "He's been busy with . . . other things. You'll bring him up to speed? Schlott wants him in proofing and canvassing. Okay?"

"Sure," Ama said.

"Thanks." With that, Challies's two companions turned and walked out. Only Challies remained, his eyes resting on Rex's. The other two Protectors moved through the crowd of ACF scouts flurrying about. They cast inspector-like glances here and there, as if checking on the scouts' progress. They didn't stop, however. They moved along distractedly, until they stepped through the hatch at the other end of the room and disappeared.

"Can I talk to you?" Challies asked Rex. Ama's eyes darted between the two.

"Yes." Rex glanced to Ama. She nodded, her eyes seeming to say, *Go ahead. You should do what he says.*

"This way," Challies said, reaching out and placing

his hand gently on Rex's shoulder. He pulled him toward the corner of the room. Around them dozens of ACF scouts were busy at work. No one seemed to be paying them any mind.

"Do this," Challies whispered. Without taking his eyes off of Rex, he reached down and clamped his palm over his own Tracker. Rex did the same. "Now stand up straight," Challies said in a clear voice. "There's nothing to hide."

Rex understood immediately that Challies was about to say something he didn't want the Ætherian Council to hear—something that they most certainly would've heard through the microphones installed on every Tracker. Rex also understood that if the two acted like they were hiding something, then they would arouse suspicion. So they needed to talk normally: one ACF Protector to an ACF recruit. That was all.

"I know who you mean," Challies said in his normal voice.

Rex was confused. "Who?"

"The person. The one you mentioned back there. The one who came up with you. *Her.*"

Rex's eyes widened. He burned with a curiosity to find her at once. He had to force himself not to whip his head around to see if anyone was listening.

"Trust me. I can help you get to her. But you and I did *not* talk, and you know nothing about me."

With that, Challies turned on his heels and followed the same path as the other two Protectors.

Rex stood in the middle of the busy ACF recruits, lost in thought. Who was Challies? What did he know? Could Rex trust him?

Trying to act normal, Rex turned around and stepped back up to the table where Ama was working. Another ACF scout of about twenty-five tapped away at a NotaScript on the edge of the table. The man's nametag read Brown 9834. Rex looked down. On the table, dozens of sheets were spread out chaotically. Rex picked one up and read:

PEOPLE OF ÆTHERIA: WARNING!

Due to heightened threats to our world's security, please be on the lookout for anyone fitting the following description:

• Unknown to you.

• Noticeably tall.

• Pale skin.

• Round eyes.

• Absence of Ætherian clothing such as AG suits and UV goggles.

• Presence of tattoos, especially the following form:

▽

• Unrecognizable accent.

If you encounter someone who meets two or more of these criteria, please message 98 23 immediately on your NotaScript. If your battery is dead, please immediately report to one of the community centers or the ACF Training Facility.

Speak only to ACF badged officials.

Treat any such individuals as **hostile**
elements and subversives.

Be alert!

Rex paused when he'd finished reading. He lay the sheet on top of the others and glanced around the table. A darker sheet caught his eye, but he couldn't clearly make out what was on it. Several other fliers like the one he'd just read were covering it. He reached over and slid the papers aside.

He gasped.

There, four or five grainy, black-and-white photo prints lay in a bundle. Rex fingered through each one. They were pictures of the bodies Rex had seen in the morgue. They were the Cthonians—the Cthonian spies that had climbed up the Proboscis tube and frozen to death in Ætheria's frigid and hypoxic atmosphere.

One picture featured a close-up of the Cthonian tattoo:

"What's all this?" Rex asked, looking up at Ama. "What's going on?"

From the corner of his eye, Rex noticed that Brown paused in his typing and lifted his head from the NotaScript. Rex didn't look, but he felt that Brown was shifting his eyes back and forth between him and Ama. Rex imagined him to be thinking. Rex felt observed, scrutinized, mistrusted . . . despite his nearly being killed down on Cthonia.

Ama demurred. She chewed her bottom lip, thinking. Her eyes locked on Rex's and flashed a spark of insight.

"We . . . the volunteers and the ACF, I mean . . . we're trying to prevent any further attacks. We have to protect our world. We have to watch out for subversives. We have to be alert. They could be anywhere. These sheets are to raise awareness of the people and keep us safe."

As Ama spoke, Rex had the impression that she was reciting some script that she'd memorized. Or that someone had *told* her to memorize. It all felt fake, contrived.

"Um," Rex said, squirming in place. He adjusted his Tracker with his left hand. "Um . . . do you know . . . " he leaned in. "Have you heard what happened down there?"

"*Like* I said," Ama snapped, cutting Rex off, her eyes glaring, "we are going to be hanging these all around Ætheria—inside and outside of every building. We have to use paper, because with the electricity cut people are soon not going to be able recharge their NotaScript batteries. No batteries, no texts, no electronic messages. You see?"

Rex straightened up. His ears rang with the hubbub of all the volunteers and scouts working frenetically around him. There was a hum to his left. He turned his head and saw that Brown was printing something from a small device plugged into his NotaScript. It looked to be another flier. The only thing different about it seemed to be the font. Rex wondered if Brown was just playing around with the fonts to make others think he was working diligently.

"Here," Ama said, looking down and removing a sheet from a scattered pile to the right of the table. She handed it over to Rex. Rex looked at the sheet.

Himmel, Rex 1421.

Canvass/Distrib. Schedule

Round 1; Morning/Pre-meal

DATE

TIME	ISLAND	BUILDING/S	LOCATION
0900	2		
0945	3		
1045	4		
1130	5		
1245	6		
1315	7		
1403	8		

"What is this?"

"Your work starts tomorrow morning," Ama said, still speaking in her almost robot-like, script-like voice. "You'll use double-sided adhesive tape to put these up on every yard and every building, and at different heights. Most people in Ætheria are staying in the community centers to stay out of the elements. There they also have water. But still, we must make sure that *everyone* knows who to look out for. The *Cthonians*. The subversives."

There was something strange about the way Ama said "Cthonians." Her voice raised and lowered quickly, as if she were speaking some secret code.

"Here," Ama continued, pointing to the bottom of the schedule. "At fourteen-oh-three, I will meet up with you on Island Eight to give you the rest of the day's schedule. When the day's work is done, you'll head back here to Bernuac HQ, where we've set up some bunks."

Rex's mind spun, but he felt Ama knew something she wasn't telling him. He wanted to ask her so many questions, but right now, with so many people around, Rex played along.

"Okay, sounds good." He nodded, looking the

paper over. "Will I be taking those?" He pointed to a neat stack of fliers at the end of the table opposite from Brown.

"Those, no," Brown said, interrupting. Rex was now certain he'd been listening to their every word. "We'll give you some tomorrow. With pictures on them. But right now I'm touching the pics up. Making them sharper. Making sure people see what they need to . . . so they'll know what to look for. We will win."

FIVE

WHILE THE WINDS HOWLED OVER ÆTHERIA, the ACF and the volunteers prepared fliers and the repair team worked feverishly to reconstruct the Proboscis and Tátea's Power Works, the Ætherian Council had called an emergency meeting.

Convening in the center room of the archipelago's Council Complex, itself located in the geographic center of the twenty-four islands, the thirty-person assembly sat around a polished circular table. Ten seats were empty. These were the ones normally occupied by the members of the Department of Energy and Survival, headed by Franklin Strapp. Because the ten members had been in Tátea's Power Works at the time of the Cthonian attack, they all had perished. And in the time since the disaster, the Ætherian Council had not yet had time to fill the vacant seats.

Seated across from the chamber's main door, Head Ductor Stan Leif fidgeted in his seat, his hands clasped in front of him, writhing in nervous tension. As head of Ætheria's three main departments—the Judiciary, the ACF, and Energy and Survival—Leif's job was to oversee the maintenance of Ætheria's survival, as well as the perpetuation of the Ætherian race. Though the members of the Ætherian Council present all held great rank over regular Ætherians, no one ever called him by his name. To all in Ætheria, he was simply the HD.

A short man even by Ætherian standards, Leif possessed big, fish-like eyes that darted around nervously, as if expecting an attack from any side. His personal oxygen tank was clasped to his back—as were all of the Council members' tanks—but the HD sucked audibly at the transparent oxygen tube that ran around his face and under his nose. If you didn't know him, you might think he was dying of some incurable lung disease; but the reality was that for the HD, pure oxygen had become like a drug. It was a drug that he insisted that all members of the Ætherian Council and Ætherian High Command have. For they—and they alone—needed to think clearly. As for the others, a permanent state of semi-hypoxia allowed them to be better controlled.

Around the table sat various other members of the Council: the Head of Judiciary; Deputy Head Schlott, the Head of the ACF; the Reviewer of New Cases; the Manager of Records and Excising; the Chief Prosecutor and Tosser; the Head of the Patrol Branch of the ACF; the Head of the Armed Branch of the ACF; the Director of Wire and Strut Maintenance; the Director of Facilities; and Ætheria's five Head ACF Protectors. Having left Rex with the workers back at Bernuac HQ, Challies strode into the room, his face flushed from hurrying over.

When the living members of the Council had all arrived, the HD began with no introduction.

"What's the news on repairs?"

The Director of Facilities stood.

"We've razed the area near the destroyed edge of Tátea," he said, looking at the HD. "My people have done a survey of the damage site and determined an area that is structurally sound enough for our next power facility. The foundation has been laid. As for the Proboscis, it is coming along much faster. We've reached fifty yards below the bottom edge of Tátea."

The HD nodded.

"With this new tube, are you going to take measures to keep another explosion from happening? What was it? Cthoneum?"

The Director of Facilities lowered his eyes for an instant and looked back up. "We're working on it."

"Do."

"Yes sir."

"And the wave of advance? The ACF?" the HD

asked, turning his attention to Schlott. "How much longer until we can descend en force?"

Schlott stood and spoke with a clear voice. "The Patrol Branch, along with several hundred volunteers, are canvassing and mounting watches for Cthonian spies." She paused and shot a knowing look at the HD. He nodded and looked into the distance. "As for the Armed Branch, they are almost ready to descend. Maybe a day or two. And we've upgraded the Stær guns. They now have a range of one hundred yards."

"Hmm. They're not going down with the full-sized pods? That would take too long."

"No. We will use the descent harnesses stored underneath each island. In the Larders. That's five harnesses per island. Those, plus the twelve full-sized descent pods, give us a total of one hundred and twenty-seven pods descending at once, each with an armed ACF regular. The plan is to descend together, secure the base of all guy wires and struts, and neutralize any Cthonians we may encounter."

"Understood. Why haven't you been able to deploy yet?"

Schlott shifted her weight from one foot to another. "Two reasons. First, we had to outfit and prep enough Stær guns for everyone. We . . . we weren't ready. We've just . . . "

"Yes?" The HD furrowed his brow.

"We've never needed that much firepower before. Our machinists have been getting the final weapons ready. When they are, we're a go."

"Humph. Lucky we haven't been attacked again while you've been dithering."

Schlott tensed her jaw. "The second reason is the Welcans cloud hasn't been calm enough. The descent pods are protected. But anyone going through the cloud in a harness is exposed. If they go through that cloud during a storm, one bolt of lightning will kill them. And then we'd have a hundred more deaths to deal with, in addition to the hundred we lost in the attack."

As Schlott spoke, the HD wagged his head with an irritated expression. "And what about the Cthonian?"

"She's stable. At your orders, her oxygen is kept low. She is too vegetative to pose any threat."

"Who's guarding her?"

"Right now, Protector Roman and two other armed ACF. But I've also assigned Challies here, who will be joining them this evening." Challies nodded at the mention of his name.

"Challies . . . " the HD repeated, lost in thought. He shook his head slowly. His eyes once again went blank, as if he were trying to remember something long forgotten. "Why aren't you with the descent force? Why aren't we sending you down?"

"My request, sir," Challies said. "I feel I'm better suited as a guard and Protector."

The HD became crimson. He turned back to Schlott. "And *you* let him?"

"Sir," she said, "Challies here *is* the highest ranked Protector we have—just one grade before being in the High Command."

"I know. Trust me, I know."

The HD sat up straight. Challies kept his eyes on the Head Ductor, who avoided returning his gaze.

"And the boy? Rex? How has his . . . performance been?" the HD snapped, looking down at the table as he spoke. Schlott had the brief impression he was avoiding everyone's eyes. She even wondered if there weren't the hint of some other emotion in the HD's voice at this question. Shame? Embarrassment? Fear? She couldn't place it.

"So far, so good," she said. "He's been cooperating. He's going out tomorrow to canvas."

"Hmm," the HD said. "I want him watched— more than just Tracked. I know things about that boy. Things you don't need to know. But watch him. I suspect that he has criminal intent. And you know what we do with criminals on Ætheria. They get Tossed. No missteps."

There was a tense silence in the room. The members of the Council kept their eyes on the HD, but few dared even to breathe. Underneath the table,

Challies clenched his fists but avoided looking at the Head Ductor.

"How much time left?" the HD finally said, looking at the Director of Facilities.

"For what?"

"How much time until we run out of water? And power?"

The Director of Facilities shifted in his seat. "Not much. Maybe a week. Maybe two. We have to hurry."

"And oxygen?"

The Council members squirmed uncomfortably. Schlott spoke up. "Sir, none of us has that information."

"Yes, yes," the HD said, looking around the circular room. Dozens of closed cabinet doors lined the walls—cabinets to which only he held the key.

"Yes, well." The HD took his chin in his hand, which was trembling. He looked around the room at the Council members present. "You should all go and warn your families. The end is close, but we're going to take drastic measures to survive. Leave the oxygen to me."

SIX

AN ALARM WOKE REX THE NEXT MORNING. HE stirred and sat up in his bunk, which was the top of three. When he'd first been assigned this bed, he'd asked for a bunk lower down, since as a child he'd often fallen out of his bed. "Sorry, that's all we have left," had been his bunkmate's answer.

Around him, fifty other ACF scouts and volunteers worked their way out of what had become an improvised dormitory. Rex glanced at the blinking red clock on the wall: 0600. Time to eat and get to work on his rounds of canvassing.

At the head of where he had slept, a packed supply

bag waited for him. It contained three hundred fliers emblazoned with the images of several of the dead and frozen Cthonians; eight rolls of double-sided adhesive; a retractable utility cutter; and a clipboard with a list of the sites he was supposed to canvass. There were three hundred in all—one for each flier. When Rex had received his instructions, he noted right away that ACF leadership had planned out the location of every flier. Pasting them inside of Ætheria's buildings would be easy enough. What worried Rex was trying to paste them outside, where the winds regularly got violent. At the end of the day, he would have to account for any lost fliers, no matter the reason. He tried to think of a way to do his work without letting the paper shriek off into the wind or becoming shredded in the gale.

Rex's first canvassing job was on Island Two—all the way on the other side of Ætheria. Even though he was to put up three hundred fliers that day, he was only one of fifty volunteers and scouts, each with the same number to post. In all, fifteen hundred anti-Cthonian fliers were going up, appearing on every wall of the stratospheric city at least three times. No two people worked together. So Rex was alone.

Because he had to cross fourteen islands and just as many Zipp lines—many of which had developed lines at their landing platforms as other scouts spread out over Ætheria's complex of islands—it took Rex just more than one hour to get to his first location: his empty house.

When Rex stepped onto the Zipp line landing pad on the north side of his island, he went through the motions of unharnessing himself. He'd harnessed and unharnessed himself so many times in his life that he could do it blindfolded. The only catching point now was a stuffed backpack strapped firmly to his back—it was filled with his fliers, adhesive, cutter, schedule, and measuring tape so that he could place the fliers exactly where they were intended.

He kept his eyes forward and directed onto the southern side of his island, where his house stood. From the Zipp line platform, its contours were invisible, but as Rex rounded the northern side of the island through the transit tube, he soon saw the familiar gray-and-white sides of the building where he'd grown up with his foster dad. A pang of fear, nostalgia, and pain welled in his chest. He'd been here just days before, but the house somehow appeared more lifeless than ever. From the outside, it seemed to emit a darkness that absorbed the energy from the houses around it. The windows were black, and even the otherwise light-colored siding had taken on a somber hue. The house seemed dead—dead, or in mourning. Rex felt a chill. It had been nearly a week since his foster dad had last crossed its threshold alive.

Before he could get too close, something off to Rex's left caught his eye. He glanced over to where Tátea's Power Works had once stood. Now, only an empty space filled the void where his father had worked. But now, it wasn't really the emptiness of the Power Works's absence that held his attention. Yes, he still felt a numb shock when he looked at where the building had been standing for his entire life. No, now what caught his eye was a flurry of activity teeming over Tátea's damaged southern edge. There, a team of at least one hundred workers scurried around like ants on an anthill. And there, hanging down about fifty yards from the island, the workers had already affixed the beginnings of a new Proboscis. The structure's surface gleamed in the morning light, and the ultra-light stratoneum that formed the tube's shell shined as if brand new.

Rex was dumbstruck. How had they rebuilt so quickly? Then he thought of the warehouse on Island Twenty-Three where he and the nine others had taken the pods down below. Images of the rows and rows and rows of massive and overly stocked shelves of parts, mechanical contraptions, and tools ran through his mind. This left him only one conclusion: the Ætherian government had already stocked replacement parts, and these allowed the ACF workers to reassemble the Proboscis so quickly, almost as if they were popping together ready-made furniture. The speed at which they had worked since the attack was mind-numbing.

Rex pulled his backpack around to his front and slipped out his schedule. His first few posts were to be within thirty feet of the transit tube's Island Two hatch. Rex removed the adhesive, cutter, and measure from his pack. He measured up four feet and ten feet away from the hatch and pasted the sheets of paper. In different times, he would've paid more attention to making the signs just level, nothing off-kilter. But now he slapped the sheets up and taped them down. He then documented the exact position of the poster: height from the ground, distance from the ceiling, distance from any other posters . . .

As he walked outside, the screaming stratospheric winds whipped at his ears and threatened to rip his backpack from his shoulders. He was used enough to walking around in this wind, but this was the first time he'd had to fight the gales to tape up paper, which hissed and snapped at the ferocious gusts. He quickly understood how this work could take all day.

Measure, position, tape, repeat. Rex soon fell into a rhythm: squeeze the open backpack between his legs, measure with his free hands, mark the place with his right hand, replace the adhesive into his bag with his left, slip out one sheet and snap it up in the softer eddy created by his body-as-wind-barrier, and tape the sheet in place. Measure, position, tape.

Rex soon lost count of how many fliers he'd taped up, but he paused when he rounded the southeast corner of Island Two. There, he stood only ten feet away from his house's dark façade.

Rex hesitated. He looked around and back at the workers on Tátea to see if anyone was watching him. No one seemed aware he was there. They were all single-mindedly focused on their work.

He took a deep breath, stuffed his fliers and tools into his backpack, and stepped up to the front door of his house.

It was unlocked.

Despite the wind's howling, which easily drowned out all but the loudest noises, Rex turned the doorknob slowly, carefully, like a burglar on edge for the slightest sound that his illicit activity might make. He pushed the door open and stepped in.

Even though he'd just been here a little more than a week before, he felt like an intruder. He was surprised to see the house exactly as he had left it. The kitchen was clean, the brushed stainless appliances shone in the dim light seeping in from outside, and the air was cold but stagnant. As he stepped in, the faint sound of his footsteps and rustling of his AG suit echoed softly off of the sterile walls.

"ALERT! ABERRATION DETECTED! ABERRATION DETECTED!"

A tinny, piercing voice burst from his Tracker, causing him to jump. At the same time, the Tracker buzzed and gave Rex a shock, like someone who'd shuffled their feet on the floor and touched him, only much stronger.

"Ow!"

His Tracker hissed and crackled. A live voice spoke to him through what must've been a tiny yet powerful speaker embedded in the device. So the Tracker was a radio transmitter as well.

"Rex Himmel, this is the ACF Monitoring Brigade. Confirm your coordinates and activity. Speak into your Tracker. You have three seconds or the shocks will increase in intensity."

A rush of panic coursed through Rex's chest and limbs. He lifted his right hand to his mouth.

"Yes, um, I'm here. Uh, this is Rex. I hear you."

"Where are you?"

"I just stepped into my house. Just to look. That's all."

"Negative. Entering your house is not part of your schedule. You are *not* to waver from your prescribed course. Ever. Not without authorization. Explain this aberration. Now."

"I was just here to look. My foster dad died in the attack. I wanted to see . . . " Rex felt his voice wavering. "I just wanted to look at my house."

A pause.

"Negative. That is not part of your schedule. You

are in violation of Ætherian Council Code Twenty-Three point Twenty-Nine dash Zero Two Four, paragraph two. This will be noted in your records and will be disseminated to Ætherian High Command. Return to your scheduled route immediately. You have five minutes for your Tracker to be detected in coordinates twelve, twenty-three, thirty-four point one for canvassing. Any deviation will result in immediate incapacitation."

Rex's heartbeat soared. He hurried toward the front door. He lifted his wrist again to his mouth as he moved.

"Incapacitation? What do you mean?"

"Your Tracker will discharge one hundred thousand volts."

SEVEN

THE REST OF REX'S ROUTE WAS MARKED BY near-paralyzing anxiety. Not the type that something is wrong, or that something bad is about to happen—it was the fear of knowing you're being watched. That every one of his moves was being monitored. And not just monitored—monitored with extreme prejudice.

Rex rushed to his next canvassing point and continued his work more feverishly than before. Like an animal being stalked, he constantly looked over his shoulder and jumped at the sign of any movement. Were those workers off on Tátea just pretending to be working? Or were they really watching him? Were invisible faces peering out at him from behind darkened windows? And more importantly: Was Rex now considered marked? A threat? If his "aberration" was being shared with Ætheria's government, would this be considered a misstep? As soon as the thought occurred, he wrestled it down. Because he knew that missteps lead to Tossings.

He had to be careful. *But if I'm that much of a threat*, he reasoned, *surely someone would be coming after me right now. But they clearly want me to keep working, so that must mean that they still trust me. At least a little bit . . .*

Rex soon got back on schedule. As he worked, he kept his eyes neurotically on his Tracker. Though he hadn't noticed it before, the device now seemed to press into his skin as if the hunk of metal and plastic were trying to burrow into him like a parasite. The Tracker stung, it bit, it itched, it throbbed. He wanted it off. But how? He shook his head. He knew that trying to force the device off might result in an electric shock, the ACF swooping down to arrest him, or both.

He continued his work.

When he'd reached Island Ten several hours later, he noticed that he could now see Ætheria's Council Complex, just to the west. Of all the twenty-four islands in the Ætherian archipelago, these were the only ones not teardrop-shaped. At the center of the Complex, one perfectly round island formed Ætheria's hub. Topped off with a stratoneum dome that shone in the blazing stratospheric sun and was only just visible from elsewhere in Ætheria, the half-spherical structure housed the one person who directed and oversaw all of Ætheria's goings-on: Head Ductor Leif. Rex had never seen the Head Ductor. Few people had.

Rex taped up the remaining fliers on Island Eight and looked at his schedule. He was on target. And he was almost finished with his morning's work. His next stop was Ætheria's temple on Island Eight to receive his afternoon's supply of fliers from Ama.

Rex Zipped across the expanse between the two islands and entered the transit tube leading to the temple's entrance. He saw no one else on the island. Perhaps Ama was already inside.

He stepped up to the temple's double doors and pushed. The right-hand door was unlocked. It swung open silently and revealed a brownish dark interior. Rex stepped in. Despite the frigid air, a dusty, stagnant smell greeted his nostrils. It was as if the building had been closed for some time—even before the attack on the Proboscis. It was as if the building itself had been lying fallow.

"Ama?" Rex called. His voice echoed in the emptiness. He looked around. The building was adorned with painted images depicting Ætherians' trinity of life and death—wind, light, and cold—along with symbols that appeared throughout the archipelago:

✿ ◇ ○

These were the three elements that all Ætherians depended on, either to stay alive or to die. The searing, stratospheric winds were a constant; and it was their unending power that led Ætheria's initial architects to design all buildings in the shape of tear-drops. In school Rex had learned about the initial buildings hundreds of years ago being ripped from the man-made, floating islands. Whoever had designed them had not considered that any flat surface facing the powerful jet stream would create enough force to uproot even the sturdiest of structures. The direct, unfiltered UV rays had, over the centuries, darkened the Ætherians' skin to a near-black color. And without wearing specialized goggles, anyone wandering outside would be blinded within minutes, their corneas burned by the sun. The cold was also not to be toyed with. Anyone not wearing their ultralight, superinsulated AeroGel suits would soon succumb to hypothermia, as the average outside temperature at this altitude was minus sixty degrees Fahrenheit. In the early decades of Ætheria's existence, the hypoxic atmosphere had led many to die from altitude sickness. But after only one generation, the Ætherians' respiratory and circulatory systems had adapted somewhat, as their blood and lungs became more efficient at extracting oxygen from the near outer-space air. Still, any effort beyond a brisk walk would lead to dizziness. That is, unless you had supplemental oxygen . . .

"Ama?" Rex called again.

A shuffle to his left caught his attention.

"Rex?" A familiar, raspy male voice answered.

Rex whirled around. Protector Challies stepped from the shadows. Rex wondered if he'd not been there all along, watching him walk in without saying anything. Challies's eyes were fixed on his. Rex had the impression that Challies was trying to communicate something to him without speaking. Now that Rex had discovered that his Tracker could also hear him and transmit messages, he understood why. Assuming, of course, that Challies had something to say that he wanted only Rex to hear.

"How did your morning go?" he asked. Rex immediately noticed that Challies spoke in a bizarre, almost programmed tone, one that reminded him of the way Ama spoke the day before. He spoke as if reciting a memorized script. He also wore a backpack—one not unlike Rex's. Rex had never seen him with this before.

"Fine. Fine. Why are you . . . ?"

"Ahem," Challies interrupted, his eyes growing wide as if to say, *Shut up!* Rex understood that Challies was up to something. "No problems?"

"No." Rex kept his answers monosyllabic.

"Really?" Challies cast an almost imperceptible glance at Rex's Tracker. Challies's tone was flat. Rex suspected the Protector knew about his going off course earlier.

"Yes. Fine. Just fine. I've finished with my fliers."

"Good. You are on schedule. Everyone else is on schedule as well. We should have the whole archipelago covered soon."

"Now what?"

Challies pulled off his backpack and shifted it to his stomach. He unzipped it and pulled out another stack of fliers.

"Here. Take these. Continue your work. It should take you about three hours to get these up. Just like the other ones. Here's your new schedule and coordinates assignment." He slipped out another schedule, identical to the one he'd used that morning. The only difference was the times and locations where he was meant to canvas. The entire schedule was printed on the front and back of one sheet of yellow paper.

"Thanks," Rex said, taking the schedule. "When can we eat?"

"When you've finished with those, at about fifteen hundred hours. Head back to Bernuac HQ then. We'll all eat there and we should be dismissed for an early evening."

"That's a late lunch, isn't it?"

"That's the schedule. We have to be attentive so that we can win."

Rex said nothing in reply. He held Challies's gaze for several seconds. Rex's eyes were inquiring.

"So," Challies said, breaking the awkward silence. "Like I said, there are your fliers. You know what to do. *There* they are." On Challies's second "there" he opened his eyes wide and stared at the stack in Rex's hands. Challies looked Rex in the eye one more time, glanced back at the stack, and tightened his jaw. "Work well. See you in a few hours. Like the others, I too have to canvass the northwestern quadrant. Your next appointment is in fifteen minutes. That might even give you a few minutes to take a peek *at these beautiful paintings* in the temple. Goodbye."

With that, Challies pushed past him and walked out. Rex followed him with his eyes. When Challies got to the temple doors, he pulled them open with both hands. They swung wide, and he disappeared into the transit tube beyond, without looking back. The doors swung closed with an empty *click*.

Rex looked at the stack of paper in his hand. *What was that all about?* he wondered. Still, Rex glanced up and saw nothing out of the ordinary: just a bunch of dusty, fake-looking paintings of the first Ætherians erecting support poles and guy wires above the clouds. There, diamonds represented the wind; circles, the cold; and a massive circle with outwardly radiating lines, the sun. He looked down.

At first glance, the fliers were identical to the others. Same images, same text, same colored paper. Without counting, he estimated there to be three hundred, like before. He gripped the stack firmly with his left hand, clamping down hard so that the sheets wouldn't drop. Like a child thumbing through an animated flip-book, he used his other hand to flip through the pages.

The pages flapped by, creating a strobe effect on the text and images. Rex saw none to be different from the others.

Then something flashed past and was gone, buried in the stack. There was something different, some other sheet of paper that had been wedged in among the fliers. Rex stopped and kneeled. He placed the stack on the floor and used both hands to sift through the pages. He worked quickly, not wanting to take too long and be caught deviating from his schedule. One misstep was enough. Page after page, he slid the fliers a few inches from the stack, revealing more and more of the dead Cthonians' faces staring blankly up at him.

And then he saw it. There, in the middle of the stack, a small folded sheet of paper about half the size of the others had been tucked in at an angle. With a pounding heart, Rex reached in and slipped it out. He unfolded it.

There, in the darkened temple, he read a handwritten note from Challies:

Trust me. They're listening. They're watching. The Cthonian is alive. You know who. She's in the Sanatorium. Where you were. She's alive, but weak. They've tortured her by suffocating her. She told them what she knew. It's all a mistake, but the HD has his own agenda. He's afraid. He wants power. He's been hoarding oxygen, and he's afraid to lose it. The truth doesn't matter. That's why they're hiding her. But she's in danger. She may be Tossed soon. You have to get to her. You are being watched. Your bunkmate and Ama are reporting on you. They're watching. If you want to get to her, you must get injured. Then they'll take you to the Sanatorium. If you just go there, they'll know. You can't get caught again. Tossings are real, and you're one step from being Tossed. They Tossed my brother years ago for no reason. This has to stop. Destroy this note when you've read it. We can't give up. I don't know how much others know. Trust me. Something big is coming. They're afraid.

Rex looked up. Fear filled his body. *The Sanatorium?* He shook his head, wondering how close his room had been to Aral's. Had that been why Schlott had acted so strangely? Had she wanted to get Rex as far away from Aral as possible, and as quickly as possible? *If only I'd known . . .* And what about Challies? Could he really be trusted? Were there others in Ætheria like him who wanted things to change? The Tossings . . . the limited oxygen canisters . . . the denials of what was happening below . . . the lies about the Cthonian air . . .

Rex looked down at the note and began to rip it into small, stamp-sized pieces, taking care not to make any noise that might be picked up by the Tracker. He buried the pieces in his fist, turned, and walked out of the temple. Once outside, he opened his hand and allowed the seventy-mile-per-hour jet stream to whip the shreds up into the sky like flakes of snow.

EIGHT

THAT NIGHT REX HAD A DREAM.
Without knowing how he'd gotten there, he was back on the surface of Cthonia. He was by himself.

For the first time in his life, he was wearing clothes other than the AG suit he'd always worn. He was wearing shorts, a T-shirt, and comfortable shoes that had a spring in their step he'd never felt before. The weather was clear and balmy; and for some reason, the Welcans cloud was no more. He looked up, and without having to worry about being burned from the intense UV rays, he saw a sky that was bluer than any he'd ever seen. It was even bluer than the skies on Ætheria, where no weather came between space and the floating city. He looked up and around, but could see Ætheria nowhere. It was like it had never existed. Either that, or he was miles and miles away. He glanced at his right arm. The Tracker was gone. He was free from the Head Ductor's prying eyes and ears.

He was free.

Up ahead, something caught his eye. It wasn't a plant or an animal, but something scraped into the sand: a drawing. As he approached, he saw that he was looking at a simple geometric shape, but one that was large, about five feet across. He drew nearer, and he soon realized he'd seen this shape before. It was an equilateral triangle bisected by a straight line:

He paused, his head down. He contemplated the drawing. Where had he seen this before? He searched his memory for clues, but his memory seemed as clear as the sky above.

Then he remembered: this was the design tattooed on the Cthonians' bodies he'd seen in Ætheria's morgue. But there was a difference. The triangles on the bodies had been inverted, their points facing down. Here, the triangle was right-side up and topped with two concentric circles. Either that, or Rex was looking at it from the wrong side. From this perspective, the triangle seemed to be forming an arrow, pointing straight ahead.

Rex walked forward, and no sooner had he taken three steps than Aral appeared. She was just suddenly there, whereas in the breath before she wasn't.

Rex walked up to the Cthonian.

"Are you better?" he asked.

She smiled and pulled her long hair behind her right shoulder. "Shouldn't *I* be the one asking you that?"

"Why?"

"You have more wounds than me."

"Wounds? What do you mean?"

"Well." Aral smiled a knowing smile. Her eyes glinted. For a brief instant, Rex had the impression that she was mocking him. But then her countenance dropped.

"Maybe I should've kept my mouth shut, after all, but they tortured me. I couldn't breathe."

"Why?"

Aral looked him straight in the eye.

"You really want to find her?" she asked, avoiding his question.

"Yes."

"Have you given this enough thought? Who knows what you might discover? What if she doesn't want to see you? You know, you should be careful what you wish for, because you might get it."

"Do you think I'm doing the wrong thing?"

"Maybe. Just don't come crying to me if things don't go your way . . ."

And with that, Aral stepped to the side and pointed behind her. Where before there had been open desert, now there was the entrance to a massive cave. But rather than the cave's mouth being open and black, it was filled with bizarre structures. The structures were clearly man-made, but they contained no right angles. There were round windows and globular doors, steps and ladders leading up and down. The whole complex looked like some giant had stuffed a wad of wax into a hole. At the bottom center of the structure, one door loomed larger than the rest. It was nearly perfectly round and was clearly some kind of main entrance—a front door.

Rex walked up to the front door. As he passed, Aral stood to the side, expressionless, and watched him walk up and open the door. He moved with smooth, even movements, like someone coming home after a long journey. He was calm and relaxed. Even though he could see nothing inside the complex, he felt no fear—only warmth and relaxation.

As he stepped in, he was greeted by an unfamiliar coolness. It wasn't like the frigid air he'd grown so accustomed to in Ætheria. No, this temperature was comforting. It offered respite from the scorching sun's rays outside.

The door closed behind Rex with a bang. He was plunged into darkness. He blinked. He rubbed his eyes. He had just seen the windows from the outside, but once inside, he could see no light. He froze. He listened. There were no sounds—not even the sound of his own breathing. But soon, he did detect a rhythmic ringing in his ears: his heart. *Babump, babump, babump* . . . the beating filled his mind and soon became deafening. Still, he felt calm.

"Rex?" A voice from behind shattered the hissing in his ears, muting his heartbeat. It was a woman's voice—one that he'd never heard before but yet knew in his heart that he had.

For the first time since he began his stroll on Cthonia, he felt fear.

"Rex, is that you?" the voice said again. Whoever she was, her voice felt both calm and accusing at the same time. *Who is that?* "Rex?" The voice cut through the darkness.

He turned around to see who it was . . .

Rex opened his eyes.

He sat up.

All around him several dozen volunteers and ACF scouts slept. A few snores combined to create a bizarre metronome that made Rex wonder if he were awake or sleeping. He glanced around from his spot in the top bunk. In the darkness of what he gathered to be the improvised dormitory in the Bernuac HQ training room, he partly expected to see the woman appear who had called to him in the darkness of the house. His hands, torso, head, and neck were covered in sweat, and his breath came in quick bursts. He tried to calm himself, to breathe silently so that he could detect all noises that crept through the room. Nothing. No woman. No voice. Only snores and sleep.

Rex closed his eyes so hard that spots, stars, and swirls danced behind his eyelids. Challies's letter swirled in his mind. His stomach cramped. His mind locked on his words. *Get injured, get injured, get injured* . . . His mother's voice echoed in his ears—that's who he'd heard in his dream. It was clear to him now. He thought about Aral, about the attack on Tátea's Power Works, about his foster dad, and about Schlott and the unseen members of the Ætherian Council who certainly had their own idea about what was happening and what had to be done about the attack from below.

Rex leaned to the side and looked over the edge of the metal frame of the top bunk. In the faint light from the exit signs ten yards away, he made out the shapeless gray of the tile floor six feet below. His vision swam. His skin felt clammy. And then, another voice echoed in his ears: that of his foster dad, who used to tease him for falling out of his bed so often when he was little. *You know, the way you toss yourself around when you sleep, one of these days you're going to fall out of your bed and kill yourself!*

Without another thought, Rex threw himself from his bunk and plummeted to the hard, unforgiving floor below.

NINE

"**W**HAT HAPPENED?"
"What was that?"
"Rex? Are you okay?"
"Aaaaahhhh! My shoulder!"

Rex writhed on the ground next to his three-story bunk. Lights flicked on in the room, bathing the still-sleeping scouts and volunteers with a bluish fluorescent glow. As Rex screamed and rolled around in agony, covers fell to the side and pillows tumbled to the ground as scouts sat up or stood to see what was wrong. Rex gripped his right shoulder and arched his back, gritting his teeth against the pain.

"My shoulder, my shoulder . . . !"

At the end of the room, the hatch flew open and Protector Roman came in. A worried look was plastered on his face.

"What's going on in here? Is everything okay?"

"It's Rex," someone stuttered. "He fell out of his bed."

"Aaaaahhhhhgggg!"

"Fell out of his bed?" Roman said in a confused tone. "What are you talking about?!" Roman shook his head dismissively and kneeled at Rex's side. A small crowd had begun to gather. Six or seven other ACF scouts formed a cluster around Rex's bunk. The scouts stared blankly at Rex, who was thrashing in pain in front of them and screaming loudly enough to be heard on all the islands of Ætheria.

"Rex, hold still for a second," Roman said, placing his hands on Rex's chest and non-wounded shoulder. "Rex . . . Rex!"

Rex gritted his teeth and looked at the ACF Protector.

"Mmm?" Rex managed to groan as an answer.

"Can I look at you? Is that okay?"

Rex nodded. Tears had welled up in his eye.

Before he proceeded, Roman turned at the loitering scouts. "Back to your bunks," he said in a calm voice. "If I need your help, I'll tell you." The scouts trickled back to their beds. "Okay, Rex, hold on . . . "

Roman leaned over and ran his hands slowly but firmly over Rex's upper torso. He inched his fingers to Rex's right shoulder. At his touch, Rex winced and fought back a scream. Satisfied, Roman sat up, his rear on his feet, which were tucked underneath him.

"I think you've dislocated your shoulder," Roman said, placing his palms on his thighs. He looked up and glanced around the room, thinking. "But it's too dangerous to Zipp across islands at night. Too much chance of a mistake. So." He stood and looked over at one of Rex's bunkmates, who was the only scout left standing near the two. With the commotion right next to his bed, he couldn't get back in and try to sleep. "You there!"

"Yes?" Rex's bunkmate stood back up.

"I need you to head to Room Twelve."

"The infirmary?"

"Yes. Go tell them we need some stratophine and a syringe. Tell them this is a code U Two-Eighty-Eight."

"Got it!" The scout turned and ran from the room. Roman looked down at Rex.

"Hang on there," he said. "We'll give you something for the pain. For now. But at first light, we've got to get you to the Sanatorium. When the medicine kicks in, which should be . . . " he looked at his Tracker, "in about twenty minutes or so, we'll need to bind up your arm to keep it from moving. Hopefully the stratophine will help you sleep."

When Rex woke up the next morning, he received another dose of stratophine. By now the pain had become a dull throbbing in his shoulder and not the searing, white-hot stabbing from the night before. He had slept surprisingly well. He attributed this to the drug.

When the second dose had kicked in, Roman got Rex to his feet and the two headed down the hall of Bernuac HQ and out the main hatch. From there, they would have to cross seven different Zipp lines to get to the Sanatorium.

Just as they reached the hatch, Rex heard footsteps running up behind him in the main hallway. He turned and saw Challies jogging toward the two. Challies's face was covered in worry, as if he'd been afraid of getting there too late. Seeing him, Rex felt a wave of relief; he wanted so badly to speak to Challies, but he knew he couldn't. Just by looking into his eyes, Rex could see that Challies was satisfied with what was happening—his plan was working. So far.

"I came when I heard. How's your arm?"

"Sore," Rex said, "but right now I'm not really in too much pain." He looked over to Roman, thanking him with his eyes for giving him the painkilling stratophine.

"Good, good. So you fell out of your bunk?"

"Yeah. It's not the first time," Rex said.

"Okay, let's go."

When they arrived at the Sanatorium about an hour later, Rex's mind quickly shifted from the pain radiating through his body to Aral. *Challies said she was here*, he thought. *But where*? They entered the transit tube leading up to the Sanatorium's main entrance. Rex became aware that if he suddenly snapped alert and inquisitive to his surroundings, Roman might notice. Given what he was learning about Challies, he wasn't too concerned about *his* reaction. Still, he had to be careful.

Rex looked at the building in front of them. Unlike the majority of Ætheria's structures, which were about a story high to better manage the high winds, the Sanatorium held at least three floors. It looked like a massive but solid blob of architecture planted squarely on one of Ætheria's largest floating islands. The island itself was a half-mile long by a quarter-mile wide.

"Ugh." He groaned when they reached the Sanatorium's door. But no sooner had he emitted his sign of pain than he wondered if he had not overdone it. Yes, his arm still hurt, but he had to figure out where Aral was. As they walked into the clinic's receiving area, he kept his left hand on his right shoulder, but allowed his eyes to lift and scan the room, the hallways, and all the doors that he could see. Like someone drunk or on the verge of unconsciousness, he tried to imagine clouding his eyes so that his peering gaze would not seem suspicious. Rather than give the impression of someone searching for clues, he hoped that people seeing him looking around would only think that he was in a delirious, painful haze.

Challies and Roman chatted with a squat receptionist behind the main counter. In hushed tones, they provided her with Rex's name and ACF identification number. Rex was struck by their complete and flawless knowledge of his entire life history. And then Rex remembered Challies's warning: *you're being watched.*

"Challies, good, you're here," someone said off to the left. Rex turned his head and saw another ACF Protector stride into the reception area. Rex didn't recognize the man, who looked to be in his mid-thirties. The man's hair was sweaty, and his eyes darted about. He fumbled with his utility belt and seemed filled with a nervous energy. Challies and Roman looked surprised at first. But as the newcomer covered the fifteen or so feet separating the reception room door to where Rex and the two commanders stood, Challies leaned over and whispered something to Roman, who nodded. Challies shot Rex a look and stepped up to the other Protector, as if trying to prevent him from getting too close—as if trying to keep him out of Rex's earshot. At the desk, Roman continued Rex's registration. But Rex kept his eyes on the two conferring men.

The newcomer was rattling off something to Challies, who nodded and looked around every few words. Rex couldn't make out the contents of what he was saying, but he could tell that the tone was tense, urgent. A few words made their way to his ears, " . . . may need your help . . . one floor up . . . security threat . . . two of you . . . stay alert in case we . . . "

"We will. Thanks," Challies finally said, placing his hand on the man's shoulder. Challies glanced once more at Rex and whispered something else to his colleague, who nodded jerkily and disappeared through the same door he'd just come from.

"This way," a new voice—a man's—spoke behind Rex. He turned around and saw a man emerge from a door just to the right of the receptionist. Rex scanned the new arrival, who was clearly a doctor. He wore blue scrubs that, because they were made of AeroGel material, hugged his body like a wetsuit. An ID badge dangled from the center of his chest. The man was clean shaven and about fifty years old.

"Left humeral dislocation suspected," the receptionist said. "I've ordered a scan."

"Thank you," the doctor said. "Hi, Rex? Welcome.

We're going to get you all fixed up." The doctor smiled, but Rex felt the smile to be forced, unnatural.

"Mm-hmm," Rex answered, his eyes drifting through the now closing door that the doctor had opened. All he saw were shelves and shelves of files, along with a few posters with what appeared to be rules and protocols for the Sanatorium staff.

"Come with me?" the doctor asked. Rex noticed that he had a distracted tone in his voice.

Rex, Challies, and Roman followed. Challies slid up next to Roman and began whispering in his ear. Rex noticed that Challies seemed unsettled by whatever the other ACF commander had told him. Was something happening in the Sanatorium? Was there a problem? Did it have to do with Aral? Where was she, even?

As the four walked down what Rex assumed to be the Sanatorium's main hall, Rex ran his eyes over each door. He remembered seeing these from before. They were all identical: dark chestnut-colored material (Plastic? Stratoneum? Rex wasn't sure), and each had a plaque affixed in the center with a number: 101, 103, 105. And on the opposite side of the hall: 102, 104, 106. A small, transparent document holder was affixed to the walls next to each door. Some contained official-looking papers stamped with the ACF seal; others were empty. Rex assumed these to be medical orders or patient cases. Every now and then, what looked like nurses or doctors strode past. Rex saw no ACF scouts or Protectors. He saw no guards. He saw no sign of Aral. And he knew it was foolish to ask.

You're being watched . . . Challies's words danced through his mind.

"Here we are," the doctor said, motioning toward a door on their left. Rex looked at the plaque. It contained no number, only a label: Intraoscular Resolution Scanner. Caution: Radiation.

Within the next few minutes, Rex found himself lying on his back on a mobile, cushioned gurney. The gurney was pointed at a massive machine of plastic and metal. The machine—the scanner—looked like an eight-foot-wide mechanical donut with a hole in the middle a yard in diameter. Rex had never seen anything like this, and he marveled at the machine, which seemed little more than a smooth, white, plastic sculpture.

As the doctor briefed Rex, Challies and Roman stood back. Like two robots with the same programming, the Protectors folded their hands in front of them. They watched intently but with empty expressions. Challies, however, was clearly nervous about something. He shifted his weight from right foot to left, and he looked over his shoulder at the closed door every few seconds.

"This machine," the doctor began, "will scan your shoulder. We need to make sure no other damage has occurred beyond a dislocation. Most injuries of this type are straightforward to diagnose and to fix. Bone pops out. We pop it back in. Done." The doctor emitted an irritating, high-pitched laugh. "But." He turned and looked at Challies and Roman as if seeking their approval. "We need to make sure there are no bone fragments or fractures that a tactile examination might not reveal. Any questions?" He looked back at Rex.

Rex shook his head.

"Okay." He took a deep breath, scanning Rex's body with his eyes. "You're ACF, right?"

Rex nodded.

"That means you're wearing a Tracker?"

"Yes." Rex lifted his right hand to show the doctor.

"That will have to come off for the scan."

"What's that?" Roman asked, stepping forward.

"The Tracker has metal in it. No metal can go through this. It's always been this way. And Rex isn't the first ACF scout we've had. Shouldn't be so surprising."

Roman shifted in place, clearly uncomfortable. He glanced at his own Tracker. He knew everything he said was being monitored.

"Rex has to wear that at all times," Roman said. "He can't remove it. That would be in violation of ACF organizational code, which states that . . . "

"I know all this," the doctor interrupted. "Yes,

I, of course, understand." He paused. He looked at Rex's arm from wrist to shoulder. He seemed to be pondering a solution. "Hmm," he said, his voice barely audible. He shook his head and looked up. "I understand the law. But the facts are these: He could have bone fragments floating around. If one gets into his bloodstream, it could make its way to his heart. That would kill him."

Rex felt a chill hearing these words. His breath faltered, and he looked up at the doctor. His heartbeat quickened. The doctor saw Rex's reaction and tightened his jaw.

"Don't worry, Rex. If there are fragments there, we can take care of them early. Then they won't cause any harm. So." He looked up at Roman and Challies. "We *have* to run the scan. He's not scheduled for a Tossing, is he? He hasn't been sentenced to death, right?"

"Well, no," Challies mumbled, glancing to Roman. Roman jerked his head in his partner's direction. Rex noticed a change in Challies's voice. It was still raspy, but it seemed strained.

"Okay then." The doctor's voice cut Challies's answer short. "So *you* don't want to be responsible for complications that this injury could create, do you? Do you want to explain what happened to your higher-ups? This is standard protocol. The Tracker comes off. We test the arm. The Tracker is back on."

"We get it," Challies said in an irritated voice. "I can take care of it," he snapped. Without waiting for Roman's response, he leaned over and pressed the tiny buttons on the Tracker's band. Rex couldn't see the order in which he pressed them, but he found it strange that Challies knew precisely the code. Or perhaps it wasn't so strange, after all . . . The Tracker beeped and unhitched. Rex immediately felt relief around his wrist. Where the Tracker had been, he felt a damp coolness as the air dried the sweat that had formed under the band. In one movement, Challies pulled the device away from Rex's arm. Even though two ACF commanders were standing over him, Rex felt freer than he had ever since he'd been conscripted into the ACF. Even though Roman's and Challies's four eyes were fixed on him, he felt unwatched. And even though their ears were capturing every noise he made and every word he uttered, Rex felt like no one was listening to him.

Challies then pulled his own wrist close to his mouth and spoke into his Tracker.

"ACF Protector Challies here, ID number 2496. I have removed Rex Himmel's Tracker for a shoulder scan." He lowered his wrist and looked around the room, his eyes wide as he awaited the answer.

There was a small pop of static, and a tinny voice emerged from Challies's wrist.

"Thank you, Challies, we hear you."

"Okay, hurry up," Challies said to the doctor. "Scan him or whatever you need to do." His eyes jumped back and forth between the doctor and Rex. Challies turned Rex's Tracker nervously in his hands.

"Thank you."

The doctor slid the scanning gurney up to the

massive, plastic-and-metal doughnut-shaped scanning machine. He positioned Rex at a ninety-degree angle to the device and eased him in. The gurney latched onto some tracks underneath, and the doctor stepped back to a panel of controls off to the side of the room. He got to work, his hands dancing across the buttons and touch screens. The machine whirred to life. The exam table moved slowly through the tube, pulled along from below. Rex felt nothing—no heat, no stinging, no gusts of air. Whatever the machine was doing to scan his shoulder, it did it invisibly, painlessly.

As Rex's head emerged from the other side of the scanner, he turned it to its side and allowed his eyes to fall on Roman and Challies. Challies was once again whispering something to Roman, who nodded absentmindedly. Challies paused, said something else, and then leaned away. His eyes seemed glassy, as if he were daydreaming.

When the scan was complete, Challies stepped up suddenly and slid the Tracker back onto Rex's wrist—but his left, uninjured arm. He pulled the two bands together and made to clip them. Working quickly, he rotated Rex's wrist so that the Tracker's latch would be facing down and hidden from view.

"There," he said, stepping back. He avoided Rex's eyes. Instead, he looked at Roman and snapped, somewhat impatiently, "He's ready. Let's get him to his room."

Rex shifted his head to watch the two. And as he did, his wrist also slid slightly against the gurney. The Tracker shifted but remained in place. Rex's breath faltered as he realized what had happened.

Challies had not reattached the Tracker.

"Okay," the doctor said, stepping back into the center of the room. "As soon as the scan comes through we . . . "

BEEP, BEEP, BEEP, BEEP, BEEP!

The doctor's voice was cut off by the shrill, piercing sound of an alarm coming from elsewhere in the Sanatorium. A small white light affixed just above the door began to flash, bathing the four in a blinding strobe. The three men jumped and looked around with worried eyes. Feeling a rush of fear, Rex leaned his head up and looked around. As he moved, he felt a shot of pain radiate from his shoulder.

"What's that?" Roman barked.

The doctor pulled a small, black device from his belt and looked down at a tiny screen. He pressed a button on the side of the device and read. He looked back up at the two men.

"Code green. The observation ward. One flight up. There's been a . . . "

"I know what it is," Challies said. He shot his eyes to Roman. "I was just told, down in the reception. It's the . . . Cthonian." He shot a glance to Rex before turning back to Roman. "She's upstairs." As before, he avoided looking back at Rex. But Rex understood: Challies had said that so Rex would know where Aral was.

"Let's go!" Challies reached over and grabbed Roman by the shoulder and pulled. The alarm continued to blare as the two Protectors pounded out of the room and down the hall. Rex could hear their running steps growing fainter. He looked at the doctor, who stood over him, immobile. The two were alone.

"What's going on?" Rex asked. The doctor looked down at his patient.

"Don't know how much I can tell you," he said. "That alarm goes off if a patient is being . . . uncooperative. Sorry about that."

An awkward pause filled the room as the alarm suddenly stopped blaring. The silence screamed in comparison to the earsplitting din. Rex looked up at the doctor.

"What next?"

"Oh, yes . . . " the doctor stepped back over to the scanner's display. His fingers danced across the keys. An image of Rex's right shoulder bones appeared on the screen. Rex squinted at the black-and-white display. He could clearly make out some of his ribs, his shoulder blade, his collarbone, and his upper-arm bone. There was a small gap in between its tip and the socket where he imagined it belonged.

The doctor peered at the image. He pressed a button, and the image zoomed in to the dislocation itself. He pressed another button and a light green outline traced the bone structures. A few little green dots blinked in the gap between the arm bone and the socket. The doctor held his finger down, and the image rotated and turned, showing the joint from every angle.

The doctor nodded his head and stepped back. He let out a barely audible, satisfied "Hmm." He turned to Rex.

"It's a clean separation. No fragments. We'll wheel you down and get the bone back in. You'll spend one, maybe two nights here. You'll need to wear a brace for a bit, but you won't need surgery. You'll be out of here soon."

TEN

AN ELECTRIC *POP* SNAPPED REX FROM A DEEP sleep.

Rex blinked his eyes open. It was dark in the Sanatorium room. He lay on his back, the purring and beeping Sanatorium filling the silence. He looked around and, through the soft red glow of the monitors to the left of his head, recognized the room: he'd been here before, just after he'd come up from Cthonia. Still groggy, he squirmed uncomfortably. His shoulder throbbed, despite his having received pain medication after his shoulder relocation. His right side felt immobilized: his upper arm was wrapped tightly against his torso, and his lower arm was folded across and wrapped around his stomach. He was wearing a lighter AG suit than what he was used to. The air in the Sanatorium still felt warm, though a bit cooler than he remembered. Rex wondered if the Sanatorium was keeping the heating low to save electricity, now that Ætheria's power source had been cut . . .

And then he remembered: Aral . . . Just before he'd put Rex asleep to reset his dislocated shoulder, the doctor had said that Rex would be in the Sanatorium overnight, perhaps even spending two nights. But that was uncertain.

What was that noise? Rex was sure he hadn't dreamt it. And what time was it? Rex looked around the room and saw no clocks. His eyelids felt sticky. His head throbbed. He glanced at the table next to his bed and gave a start. There, next to two bottles of medicine, his Tracker lay dormant, its band reattached as if it were on display in some store. Its red light blinked every few seconds, indicating that it was functioning normally. *Strange*, he thought, remembering that Challies had put it back on his arm after the scan. But he hadn't fastened it. *Who took it off?* Mesmerized, he watched the regular flashes. *Did the ACF think the Tracker was on him? What was going on?* He looked closer and realized that a piece of opaque tape had been affixed to the underside of the Tracker's body. *That wasn't there before . . .*

The door clicked and opened. Rex looked up. It was Challies.

Moving heavily, clumsily, the ACF Protector backed into the room, bent over something he was dragging across the floor. Rex strained to see what it was, and was astonished to see the uniformed body of an ACF Protector. As Challies worked his way in, Rex saw that it was Roman.

Challies slid his colleague all the way into the room and lay him down gently. Roman stirred and let out a soft snorting sound. He wasn't dead, just asleep. But why? And then Rex thought of the electric *pop* that had woken him up.

"Challies . . . ?" Rex said, his voice heavy with sleep.

"Shhh," Challies answered, sliding up to the bed. He paused over Rex and eyed the patient from head to toe. He seemed to be deciding what to make of Rex . . . as if he had a plan to share but suddenly had his doubts. His eyes fell on Rex's Tracker. He looked back and forth between the Tracker and Rex. He then took a deep breath and leaned in so close to Rex that his lips almost touched Rex's right ear— the one opposite the side where the Tracker lay. Rex instinctively pulled away, but Challies reached over and pulled his head back to his mouth. Rex could smell Challies's breath.

"Listen," Challies whispered so softly into Rex's ear that Rex had to concentrate to understand what he was saying. He then realized that Challies was speaking this way to avoid his voice being detected by Rex's Tracker or his own. Rex focused on the Protector's words. Maybe now he was going to find out what Challies meant.

"Quiet," Challies said. "I only have a few seconds. Roman was stationed at your door as a guard. He is dazed, but he'll wake up soon. I hit him with my Stær gun from behind. He didn't see me.

"I know why you're here. I know your fall wasn't an accident. So does the Head Ductor—he knows you're trying to get to Aral, and he wants you to make a mistake. I think he really wants you Tossed.

"Here, I'm assigned to guard the Cthonian. I left my Tracker in her room, so they think I'm there. I put tape on yours and mine. That way the skin sensors won't think the Tracker's off. All they look for is a surface that's up against the Tracker.

"If you want to save her, and save yourself, you need to go. Now. They're going to Toss you if you don't. Trust me. I've seen this before. I can distract the others long enough. You should be able to get into her room. It's upstairs. But you have to hurry."

Challies leaned back and looked Rex in the eye. Rex furrowed his brow and mouthed the word, "Why?" He mouthed slowly and clearly, hoping that

Challies would understand. The Protector leaned in and whispered again.

"Ten years ago, they Tossed my brother. For no reason. Just some stupid suspicion. They killed him. The HD's paranoia is out of hand. He thinks everyone's after the oxygen. He thinks it's his. And now he's worried about you. He's *afraid* of you. He also knows about your mother down in Cthonia. He thinks you're working with her. You've already broken the law once. If you don't save the Cthonian now, they'll let her die. Like the others you saw in the morgue. They've already Tossed two other Cthonians. I was there. The HD thinks they want war. Now he thinks you're a spy. You're in danger. You need to flee. Get the Cthonian and go back down!"

Rex pulled his head away. "What?! That's insane! Why would he think all that?"

Challies shook his head. "No time to talk now. Just know that he does, and he can't be trusted. You've got to get out of Ætheria. Now."

"But the Cthonians shot at us down there," he mouthed. "My team was killed."

"You'll be killed if you stay! Don't you get it?! I'm sure of it. They've already got you under guard. What next?"

Rex felt his heart beat faster and his palms go sweaty. "What do we do?"

"Come with me," Challies said. "I'll get you to her room. Then you both need to get to the descent pods and get down. It's the only way. Come on! But don't make any noise!" He pointed at Rex's Tracker to remind Rex they were still being monitored. Rex nodded.

With leaden legs, Rex worked his way up and shifted his feet off of the left side of the bed and to the floor. Despite having been anesthetized for his arm relocation procedure, he felt surprisingly lucid. As he moved, Challies took his arm and lifted, helping him stand. The Protector's arms were muscular. Rex leaned against them as he moved.

Trying to avoid making noise, Rex massaged his

right arm, which protruded from the sling hugging his right arm and body. His right hand felt clammy and cold, as if the circulation had been cut off. He wiggled his fingers to make sure. He felt no numbness, no tingling.

Rex and Challies inched toward the door. Rex's socked feet made no noise as he moved across the linoleum floor. The two gingerly stepped around Roman, who snored as if lost in a pleasant dream. Challies pressed his ear against the door and listened. From the hall outside, only the sounds of rushing air, the occasional footstep in the distance, and a low, mechanical hum worked their way to the Protector's ear. He turned and nodded to Rex. Challies then eased his hand to the metal doorknob and applied pressure. With a soft *click* that made Rex's nerves jump, the Sanatorium room door opened and glided inward, revealing a dimly lit hall outside.

"Let's go."

Challies opened the door all the way and pulled Rex out into the hall with him.

Following Challies's lead, Rex looked in both directions. He recognized the nondescript, numbered rooms from before. Off to the right, the hallway continued for another fifty feet or so before turning to the right. To the left, about a hundred feet away, the fluorescent blaze of ceiling lights created a glowing bastion where four nurses or doctors huddled around a desk, chatting. They faced each other, engrossed in something they were reading on the desk. Their backs were turned to Rex and Challies.

This was their chance.

Before moving down the hall, Challies turned and closed the door behind them. *Click.* Rex's heart leapt into his throat at the sound. He jerked his head in the nurses' direction. They hadn't noticed. He turned his back to them, and the two began to move their way down the hallway. They shuffled along quickly. As they moved, Rex kept his eyes on the room numbers, which were just barely visible in the gloom.

"She's upstairs," Challies whispered. "There." He nodded straight ahead. At the end of the hall a glowing sign cast out green light from above a door one hundred feet away: stair.

The two pushed forward. As they moved, Rex was relieved to feel his energy returning, as if by moving he was waking up his limbs, body, and mind.

When they reached the entrance to the stairway, Rex cast a nervous glance behind him. No one. He had no idea how frequently the nurses did their rounds, but surely it couldn't be more than every fifteen minutes or so. And when had they done their last round? What would happen if they did a round and saw that he was no longer in his room? And found Roman unconscious on the floor? Surely they would sound an alarm. They had to hurry.

Challies pushed the stairway door in. The metallic *clank* of the door's latching mechanism echoed up and down the stairwell walls. At the noise, the two whipped themselves into the stairwell and eased the heavy door shut behind them. For a good thirty or forty seconds, they stood unmoving against the cool wall, listening for any unusual sounds.

Nothing.

One flight down, another green light shone from above another door: exit. As in the hall, the stairwell's only light came from this door light. Rex wondered if the Sanatorium was keeping so many lights out to conserve energy in the wake of the Power Works's destruction. That had to be it. Why else would everything be in the dark?

The two headed up the stairs to the next floor. When they reached a doorway marked only with a large black 002, Challies listened, eased the door open, peeked out, and froze. Rex leaned over so that he could see beyond Challies's shoulder.

Unlike the last hallway, this one was bathed in light—and not just enough light to allow nurses and doctors to find their way around. The light was blinding and made Rex's eyes smart as he peered in from the comparatively black stairwell. He felt as though he were looking at an overexposed picture, one in which all color was washed out by an overabundance of powerful light bulbs. Through his watering eyes, Rex saw no one, but he was physically stunned—both by the light itself and the heat radiating out of the hallway and into the stairwell . . . no doubt a result of the glaring ceiling lights chasing away any hint of darkness.

Moving quickly, the two stepped into the hallway and slid their way down the corridor. The passage was little more than a series of unmarked, identical doors, each hiding something unknown, something mysterious.

Halfway down the hall, Challies paused. He looked and listened. Rex's heart throbbed in his neck and in his temples. Sweat ran down his forehead and into his eyes. His hands were clammy. He was suddenly overcome by an uncanny—no, an unnatural—feeling, almost as if he were being watched. Instinctively he reached his left hand to his right wrist. No Tracker. He realized he felt almost naked without it.

Rex looked up. There, at twenty-foot intervals, a series of shoebox-sized plastic canisters were attached to the junction of the ceiling and the walls. Shaped like miniature caskets, the surface of the boxes facing the hallway were of a different material. The boxes were sealed with gold-tinted two-way mirrors—slates of semi-reflective glass that no doubt housed security cameras.

Rex *was* being watched.

But, he thought, *if they can see me, why is no one coming? Why are there no alarms?* He then realized that doctors, nurses, or the ACF would only come if they actually saw him—in other words, if they were actually watching the monitors that were connected to these cameras. He thought of the nurses he'd just seen. None seemed to be doing their work. They'd been chatting. Rex hoped that any other staff in the building would be just as distracted.

"There," Challies whispered, pulling Rex to the side of the hall and up to a door as equally ordinary as the others. "She's in there. I'll stand out here. I'm supposed to be on guard. But remember: my Tracker is in there, so hand it to me right away so you can't be monitored. It's on the table beside her bed, like in your room. And hurry! Any minute, Roman will wake up or a nurse will check on your room. Get her, get out, and get down! Here." Challies fished in his pocket for something. He pulled out a Nanokepp Card. "This is my card." He handed it to Rex. "It will get you across the Zipp line and into the warehouse where the descent pods are. You were there before! It should be closed and locked at this time of night, but this will get you in. You've used them before, so you should know how to get down. That's your only chance, but you've got to hurry!"

With that, Challies opened the door and pushed Rex inside. A surge of nervous energy flooded Rex. He closed the door behind him and faced the bed. There, lying in a mass of restraints, wires, and tubes, Aral opened her eyes and faced Rex.

ELEVEN

HOLDING HIS FINGER IN FRONT OF HIS MOUTH for her to be quiet, Rex slid up to the Cthonian's bed and carefully lifted Challies's Tracker from the bedside table. He noticed that Challies's device also had a piece of opaque tape across its back. *Silly*, he thought, *something that technologically advanced and you can trick it with something that basic.* Sliding carefully in his socked feet, he opened the door and reached out. Challies took the device and slid it into the pocket of his AG suit. He didn't put it back on his wrist. He then looked Rex in the eye and mouthed, "I've got to get out of here, too."

"Come with us," Rex mouthed back. Challies shook his head.

"I have to distract them—throw them off your trail. Just go!"

Before Rex could respond, Challies grabbed the door handle and eased it shut. Rex returned to the bed.

"Aral?" he whispered. Before she could answer, Rex scanned the spaghetti-like tangle of plastic coursing over her. Her arms, legs, and torso were immobilized by wide, synthetic-hooked cloth belts. No locks held Aral down. She wore a surprisingly large AeroGel suit, similar to Rex's. *Where did they find one so big?* Then he noticed as he stepped closer that her suit seemed hastily stitched together from the pieces of many others.

An intravenous tube stretched upward from her clothed left arm, a small portion of which had been left exposed to allow access to her artery. But the fluid dripping into Aral's veins was not clear, as Rex's had been. It was milky—opaque, even. The drips plopping down from the main IV bag and into the drip chamber reminded Rex of concentrated soap, the kind his foster dad used in the kitchen for the dishes. A foggy, thin plastic hose ran over Aral's face and under her nose, where two smaller outlets disappeared into each nostril. Two straps around her ears held the hose in place. Rex followed the tube away from Aral and to the cluster of machines and apparatus to the right of her bed. There, it was latched to a five-foot-tall oxygen canister. And then Rex understood. *Without extra oxygen, she'd die. Just like those spies that had come up. She can't breathe up here.* The gauge on top of the oxygen tank read O$_2$SAT 70%.

Seventy percent? How can she survive? Rex knew that anything below eighty-five percent oxygen saturation in any normal human would spell hypoxia, coma, and death. *What's happening?*

"Aral?" Rex repeated. He placed his hand on her forearm and withdrew it as if he'd just burned himself. Her skin felt cold, clammy—dead, even.

Aral turned her eyes toward him. She blinked

slowly, deliberately, as if trying to communicate with her eyes, which Rex noticed were hazy. She nodded.

"What is it?" Rex asked. "Can you hear me?"

Aral nodded. Rex thought he caught a glimmer in her eye—one that hadn't been there just seconds before. But she remained silent.

"Can you speak?"

Aral eased her head side-to-side. *No.* She blinked once again and lifted her eyes toward the oxygen tank. Or at least that's what it looked like she was looking at. Rex stepped over and looked more closely at the machine.

At its top, the metal container tapered into a point. But before becoming a true point, the tank was topped with a valve hookup, the monitor, and a valve protruding from the right side. Rex leaned in and squinted his eyes. Though it was dark, he didn't want to take the risk of turning the room's light on. First, he didn't know if the lights were monitored some-where. And second, he didn't want to risk someone seeing the light from underneath the door, despite the blinding light filling the hallway and Challies being stationed just outside.

Rex hovered in front of the machine, his eyes fixed on the valve. Slowly, too slowly, his eyes adjusted to the dark. What had first appeared to be a plain round knob revealed a colored wheel that faded from light to dark. In the dim glow of the red monitor lights, Rex couldn't tell what colors the knob truly was. But within the next minute, several numbers circling the knob's perimeter became clear, as did the oxygen tank's setting:

```
O₂ output 0%---30%---|||---60%---80%---100%
```

Rex stood up and looked at Aral. As the truth became clear, he reached out without thinking and grabbed the knob. Whoever was monitoring her had set the oxygen at half its output capacity. But had they done it on purpose? Or had it been an accident? Because at this level of oxygen, Aral was being held in a state of hypoxia. She was oxygen-deprived.

Rex turned the knob to one hundred percent.

The tank let out a whining hiss before settling into a softer *shhhhhhhhhhh*. On the bed, Aral tilted her head back slightly as if trying to pull her nose away from something unpleasant. The sound caused Rex to spin around in fear. He was sure someone outside had heard and would be barging in any second. *Surely these oxygen tanks are monitored.* He stepped to the door and listened. Nothing. But his panic only grew. He knew a nurse would have to come by any moment to check on the patients. Perhaps then Challies could offer a distraction?

Rex walked back up to the bed and looked down. In the few seconds since he'd increased her oxygen flow, Aral's eyes had cleared. They once again looked alert, intelligent, piercing—just as he'd seen down below . . . down on Cthonia. As the oxygen flowed and hissed, her chest heaved with deep, filling breaths. In the gloom, Rex swore he could see color returning to her features, despite Cthonians' natural pallor. She wiggled her fingers, and Rex could sense the energy returning to her limbs along with the life-giving oxygen.

Without speaking, Rex reached across and began unbuckling Aral's straps: first her hands, then her feet. With each clank and rustle, his nerves jumped. *Had someone heard? Was anyone coming?* But he moved quickly—frenetically yet in control. He breathed quickly, and sweat covered his brow. As he finished unstrapping Aral's remaining foot, she reached up and unfastened her torso restraint. And in the next second, she was seated upright. Rex stepped back, his eyes fixed on Aral as if he hadn't seen her for weeks, when in reality it had only been four days.

"Thank you," Aral said in a clear voice. The weakness had disappeared. Rex was stunned at how fast her strength was returning. Then he remembered how strong he'd felt back on Cthonia, when his mask had been ripped off. Within seconds of breathing in the dense Cthonian air, he had felt more filled with life than he'd ever been on Ætheria. It was amazing how powerful air was to someone suffering from hypoxia. It was like a fast-acting drug.

Looking at Aral, Rex was overcome by a surge of questions.

"What happened?" was all he could manage. As his voice broke the silence, he looked over his head like a pursued hare expecting to be caught by a hawk. Rex turned back to Aral. "Have you been here the whole time?"

Aral shook her head. "No. First they asked questions. Many questions. They turned my oxygen off. They . . . "

"Shh!" Rex interrupted. "You can tell me later. We have to get out, now," Rex said, his eyes jumping to Aral's IV and oxygen machine. His head jerked about. He was clearly in a mounting panic.

"Get out?"

Rex stopped probing the room with his eyes and faced Aral. "Something's going on. They're keeping your oxygen low on purpose. They're trying to cover something up—hide something. And . . . " He paused, musing. "If the Head Ductor is behind all this, there's no way we're going to get to whoever it is to talk any sense into them. If *you* don't get out of here, then they're going to just strap you back down and turn down your oxygen . . . if they don't turn it off completely. We're in danger, and we've got get out of Ætheria. And I've got to find my mom."

"How?"

"We've got to get back to the descent pods. Let's just hope that whoever's down there will let us explain ourselves before shooting at us."

TWELVE

CHALLIES HAD TO HURRY.

Nurses in the Sanatorium made their rounds every fifteen minutes. Challies didn't wear a watch, but he knew at least ten minutes must've passed since he stunned Roman, who'd been guarding Rex. It would be just minutes before a nurse made a round to Rex's room and saw that his guard was gone and, if they opened his door, that Roman had been attacked. When that happened, an alarm would be sounded. And he knew that once the alarm rang, a team of ACF scouts would swarm the Sanatorium Complex, if not the entire Ætherian archipelago.

And what would happen when the Ætherian Council realized his role in the escape? He knew they'd immediately suspect him when they found Roman. He knew they'd start a search for him, too. He knew he was about to become a fugitive, and he had little doubt what would happen to him once the ACF caught up with him.

He would be Tossed, like his brother before him.

Challies glanced around up and down the hall. He was alone. With heart pounding, he took a deep breath. Another.

Then he ran down the hall toward the stairwell and, without hesitating, pushed the exit door open and stepped outside. The frigid, stratospheric winds greeted him with a skin-piercing howl, making the exposed skin on his face tingle.

He looked around. It was still dark, but he imagined dawn wouldn't be long coming. All around, the Sanatorium Complex was empty. The dim light of the moon revealed the soft glow of the turf pathways and enclosed transit tubes that circled every building and island in the Ætherian archipelago. He paused, watching, listening. He opened his eyes wide, swearing at them under his breath to adjust to the dim light.

As the building and pathway became clearer, he shuffled off to the right, keeping the Sanatorium within arm's reach. He put about fifty yards between himself and the exit door, before stopping and slipping his hand into his AG suit pocket. His Tracker was still there.

This was his only chance for throwing off the ACF. Knowing they monitored the device's movements, Challies plucked his Tracker out of his pocket and hurled it as hard as he could over the top of the Sanatorium building, where it banged and clanked before sliding down the other side. As soon as a nurse found the unguarded doors and Roman's unconscious body, the search would begin. Not finding him, the ACF would suspect Challies right away. They'd call in a report. And Bernuac HQ would immediately inform them of the Tracker's location—away from Rex and Aral. The ACF would be thrown off for at least enough time for Rex and Aral to get to the descent pods.

Or so he hoped.

Now what?

There was no way he could get to the warehouse and the descent pods. He shook his head in frustration. Now that Rex had his Nanokepp Card to cross over to the secure island, the only way he'd be able to follow them would be to scramble across the wire, holding on with his legs and arms. With the wind as strong as it was, and with the temperatures as low as they were, doing that without a harness would be suicide—and he needed his Nanokepp Card for a harness. He'd fall. And even if he didn't fall, getting across would take far more time than he had.

Challies looked at the Sanatorium. He rushed back to the door they'd used. Hide in there? Head back to Aral's empty room and hide over the ceiling until things calm down? Had they even made it out? No, too risky. As soon as the ACF examined the empty rooms for clues, some other patient would be put there, and it would be impossible to get out without being spotted.

Challies clenched his fists and let his eyes drop.

And then he saw it.

Just more than ten feet in front of him, a circular manhole cover rested on the ground. Challies could just make out its black form in the light of the unobstructed stars and waning moon. Lucky it wasn't the full moon. Judging by the moon's size, the sky would be almost completely dark two days later. But now, what was left of the moon revealed the island's Larder—the hollow space underneath the man-made ground that held backup supplies for the inhabitants in case of emergency: Self-Contained Respirator Masks, AG suits, LED lights, goggles, and, more importantly, food and water.

Seeing the portal made all of his other thoughts vanish. He forgot about the Sanatorium, he forgot about the Zipp lines, he forgot about the future. Right now, he needed to get hidden, and fast. The Larder would allow him to stay hidden for several days at least. He was no longer wearing his Tracker, so no one would know he was there. He would just have to hope no one would think to look here once the search began. Hopefully the ACF would assume he'd gone down with Aral and Rex. After all, there would be a record of his Nanokepp Card being used to cross the Zipp lines to the descent pod hangar . . .

All he had was hope.

Challies lurched forward and threw himself on his knees. Before now, he'd never opened a Larder on his own, but he'd seen it done. He fumbled in his belt for his multiuse utility knife. Working against the cold biting into his bare hands, he pulled out the knife, opened it, and unfolded it to reveal a pry blade. He jammed the blade in between the manhole cover and its cement frame. He twisted and pried. The thick, round slab of metal scraped and shifted in place. He pushed down hard on the top end of the knife's handle. Inch by inch, the cover lifted, until a space wide enough for his fingers appeared between the black metal and the hole itself. With rapid, shivering breaths, he thrust his fingers through, latched onto the cover's underside, and pulled. The metal slab must've weighed forty pounds—heavy enough to cause his fingers to strain, but not heavy enough to slam shut, pinching them from his hand.

With a grunt, he pushed the manhole cover to the side, revealing a gaping black hole beneath. Challies slid forward and plunged his legs into the darkness, reaching with his feet for the ladder he knew to be there. When his foot found purchase, he shimmied down into the hole, stopping just as his eyes were level with the ground. Sliding his knife back into his pocket, he latched on with his legs and reached up with both arms, grabbed the slab cover, heaved it back into place, and ducked, letting the ponderous metal circle thump closed over the hole, leaving him buried alive in the freezing dark.

Just as the Larder closed, the Sanatorium's alarm sounded.

THIRTEEN

BEEP! BEEP! BEEP! BEEP! BEEP!

Aral and Rex jumped at the piercing sound of an alarm . . . the same one he'd heard before. The same white light bathed the room in a washed-out strobe. Every muscle in Rex's body tensed. His skin tingled with fear. Aral stood and reached for the oxygen tank. With one powerful yank of her left arm, she pulled it over to her with a clank.

"They're coming," she said.

Rex's eyes flew to Aral's bed, where five sets of straps lay crisscrossed over the rumpled white sheets.

"Did we set it off?" He pointed to where she'd been lying. Aral shook her head.

"No. Someone pressed that." She pointed to a red button to the right of her bed's metal headboard. Rex recalled seeing it in his room, but he had not registered what it had been. "Someone must've set it off. In another room. That happened before. But here."

As she finished her sentence, the sound of dozens of stomping feet added to the sound of the alarm. People were running one floor below them . . . it sounded as though the hall was overflowing with clumping, angry boots. Rex froze, listening. The steps were moving away from their room and down the hall—down to where the hall angled ninety degrees and stretched away . . . toward Rex's room.

"They must've found Roman!"

"I can't take this with me!" Aral said, her voice almost a shout. She motioned to the bulky oxygen tank to which she was still attached and to the IV line, which dug into her arm. Rex looked at the tank and guessed that it must've weighed at least sixty or seventy pounds.

"We don't have any choice," he said, pointing at the plastic tubes stretching from her arm. "We've got to pull them out and try to find the hatch . . . without oxygen. We'll have to hurry!"

Aral nodded and looked at her left arm, where the IV's needle lay buried in her vein. She scanned the setup quickly and then reached over with her other hand and gripped the tubes. Rex saw her tendons tighten in her hand as she gripped . . . and pulled.

Without a sound, the IV drip tube popped off, leaving a trail of milky white drops across Aral's arm. The tube flopped down, where it hung flaccid at the bed's side. A steady stream of white drops plopped to the linoleum floor.

Rex didn't have much time to admire Aral's work. No sooner had she pulled the tube from her arm than a fine but powerful spurt of blood hissed out from her vein. With each heartbeat, a spray of bright arterial blood launched out several feet, sending a crisscross pattern of speckled crimson across the floor and bed. When she'd pulled off the tube, Aral had left the hypodermic needle in. If they didn't do something immediately, she would bleed to death.

"Ugh." Aral groaned, standing. Moving with precision, she pinched the exposed part of the needle between her thumb and forefinger. Her fingers slipped across the growing swath of blood on her forearm. She tried again, pinched, and yanked. Rex glimpsed a silver flash between her fingers as her bloodied hand pulled away. She flicked the needle across the room. A faint metallic tinkle echoed across the floor. Aral pushed her hand against her bloodied arm to stop the blood flow. Her eyes darted to the oxygen tank.

"Do you think you can get us over there?" she asked.

"I'll have to. You won't have much time without oxygen."

Downstairs, shouts echoed through the Sanatorium

halls. More footsteps thundered. *They've found Roman. They know I'm gone.*

Aral took in one final deep breath, the sound of the oxygen hissing through her nose tube. She reached up and pulled the clear plastic tube from her nose and over her head. She tossed it over to the oxygen canister, where it got hung up on the knob Rex had turned.

"Let's go," she said. "I don't want to die up here."

Moving quickly, Rex eased Aral's door open and peeked out. He was stunned to see that Challies had left. Why? And then the most logical answer struck: he must've run downstairs to help with the "search" for Rex. With any hope, he was delaying the other ACF troops or throwing them off the trail.

Rex squinted at the bright lights filling the hall with their fluorescent glow. He looked left and right. Far down to the left, he saw the shadows of what must've been nurses or doctors—or maybe ACF scouts?—bustling about near the nurses' station. Aside from that, the hall was empty. He held his breath and listened. Shouts pushed up through the floor below. He strained to understand the words, but they were just a muffled, garbled murmur. He listened for Roman's or Challies's voices, but couldn't tell who was speaking. Whoever it was, he was certain that the voices must've been those of ACF officers or scouts.

"C'mon," he whispered, pulling Aral into the hall. Still in socked feet, he slid-ran across the polished linoleum toward the stairs he'd just taken . . . and where he'd seen the exit. When he reached the heavy door, he pushed, and the two stepped into the cavernous, echoing stairwell. Walking on the balls of his feet, he bounded down one flight of stairs and paused in front of the exit, whose beckoning light filled the gray concrete walls with an otherworldly green. He placed his hand on the door and turned to Aral.

"We have to hurry outside," he said. "It'll be cold. But it shouldn't be that hard to find. When we get out, let's turn left and work our way around the building. We've got to get to the warehouse where the pods are."

Aral nodded. Rex had the impression that she was trying to conserve oxygen by not speaking.

"Okay!" Rex whispered and pushed against the door.

Adrenaline and panic surged through Rex . . . so much so that he couldn't tell if the tingling he felt throughout his body was due to the cold or fear or both. Behind him, Aral emitted a groan that sounded like one of pain or terror. She placed her hand on his shoulder and pushed, urging him on.

The two burst into the night, letting the door slam behind them.

Before Rex had taken three steps, his feet howled in pain. Wearing only the Sanatorium's socks, his feet were unprotected from the frigid temperatures, which he'd remembered hearing once as fluctuating between negative forty and negative sixty degrees Fahrenheit. If they didn't get across the Zipp line and to the warehouse soon, his feet would surely freeze. He ran forward, trying to wiggle his toes with each step. Behind him, Aral ran with high knees as if each step burned her feet. Fortunately both of them wore the Sanatorium's tight AG suits, which protected their bodies, but not their feet. Images of the frozen Cthonian spies flashed through Rex's mind. *Step, step, step* . . . with each footfall, Rex felt his feet become heavier, as if weights were strapped to them. But he mustn't stop moving, no matter what.

With the siren wailing through the night and the wind whipping around them, the two plodded through the dark toward the Zipp line platform, which lay fifty yards to their left. If they could reach it and cross, they might have more of a chance to make it across the others standing between them and the warehouse. Rex kept his eyes on the ground at his feet, while Aral kept her eyes on Rex's back. At this height, no clouds obscured the crescent moonlight, which cast an eerie bluish glow across the rounded Sanatorium building and the turfed ground. Rex sped to a run; he didn't sprint outright, because he wanted Aral to be able to see and follow him. He also didn't want to take the risk of blacking out himself, which is what would happen if he moved any faster than a fast walk.

As things were, he could no longer feel his feet. With each step, tears stung his eyes. He tried to keep wiggling his toes, but he couldn't tell if they were responding. His feet were little more than heavy masses of flesh carrying him along.

Just as they rounded the building's corner where the wind dropped off, Aral's hand came down hard on Rex's wounded shoulder. He shouted in surprise and pain, as the jarring shook his bound shoulder, which still smarted.

Rex turned to face Aral. In the moonlight, he could see that her face, arms, and shoulders were drooping. The expression had left her eyes. She looked like someone who was either drunk or gravely ill. Her mouth moved to speak. Only garbled words dripped out. She shook her head, realizing the sounds she was making were not what she was intending to say. She tried again.

"Ummghghg . . . "

Rex reached forward with his good arm and slid his hand under her armpit. He tried to pull her up, but she was little more than dead weight. He was surprised at how heavy she was. For some reason, he'd never equated her taller height with greater weight. He realized that she must've weighed at least fifty pounds more than he. He pulled again, twisting his body and grunting with effort. The strain pulled at his wounded shoulder, causing him to grimace in pain.

"Aral! Are you okay?"

"Ummggg . . . " she mumbled, her mangled words ending in a hiss.

Oh, my God. She's running out of air.

He glanced down at her feet, which were bent toward each other at an unnatural angle. Rex could no longer feel his feet. Surely she felt the same thing.

"Spread out! Search the perimeter!" The wind, though calmer on this side, carried these two deadly orders across the Sanatorium's rounded surface and to where Rex and Aral stood. A volley of "Yes!" and "Check!" echoed back. The ACF troops were outside and surrounding the building, looking for the two fugitives. Aral lifted her head groggily. She'd heard them as well, but she seemed unable to react, beyond merely shifting her position.

In his panic, Rex no longer felt the pain firing up from his feet. Screaming with effort and the agony of his newly relocated shoulder bones grinding against each other under his brace, he clamped his hand onto Aral's right arm and rotated his body, positioning her onto his back. Like a fireman dragging a victim from a raging inferno, he flexed his leg muscles and trudged his way forward, with Aral's body weight pushing down on him. Against the cold, the wind, the dark, the oncoming frostbite, and the numb ache in his right shoulder, Rex covered the last twenty yards to the Zipp line platform. With each step, his thighs screamed from the effort, and he felt that his feet might give way any second. But he couldn't afford to stop now. Getting caught straying from his canvassing route and walking into his deserted house may have warranted a warning, but there was no doubt in his mind that escaping from the Sanatorium with Aral—a declared enemy of the state—would be the last straw. His dad's stories of the Tossings echoed in his mind with each step. And now he had Challies's story about his brother to add to the mix. When the pain became too much to bear, he envisioned Ætherians being thrown alive over the edge of the islands, their screaming and flailing bodies hurtling into the Welcans cloud below, never to be seen again. Each time this image flashed before his eyes, he managed the strength for several more steps.

"This way!" someone shouted from behind. Other voices echoed from the opposite side of the Sanatorium. The scouts were getting closer.

Rex's breathing now came in wheezing gasps. Having grown up in Ætheria, he was used to the rarefied atmosphere, but the effort and pain of Aral's weight, his shoulder, and the cold on his feet was straining his body and mind to their breaking point. His face was twisted and covered in sweat, despite the frigid air. His left arm and hand trembled from the effort of holding the limp Cthonian across his back. Aral's head lolled on his right shoulder, sending new jolts of pain through his arm. Her breath sounded weak; he knew she'd pass out soon. And if that happened, she'd soon die. As he worked his way forward, he cursed himself for risking her life in this way. *Why did I bring her out without oxygen? Why run away like this?* He thought about trying to escape with the massive oxygen container. Fleeing without it had been a necessary risk . . . but one that was about to cost them both their lives.

When he felt he could carry her no more, he planted his numb socked feet on the stratoneum platform of the Zipp line. He worked quickly. He reached up and pulled the harness down with his good arm.

"Aral, you've got to put your feet through this!" he screamed over the wind. The Cthonian responded with a moan, pushing against his shoulders to lift her legs one after the other into the nylon strap. Rex groaned at the increased pressure on his wounded shoulder, but adrenaline helped him to power through the pain. One leg, then two . . . With both of her legs in the harness, Rex buckled the device in front of her stomach and looked behind him. From around the side of the Sanatorium fifty yards away, a dazzling display of white headlights danced as ACF troops neared the corner. They were still hidden by the building, but Rex could see by their lights that they would be upon the two fugitives in seconds.

He turned back to the Zipp line and pulled Challies's Nanokepp Card from his pocket. *What to do?* There was no time for him to harness himself in. And he didn't trust his own strength to cling onto Aral's back as she Zipped across.

Panic-stricken, he looked back at the Sanatorium and saw the furious silhouettes of the ACF rounding the building.

"Check the Zipp line!" someone shouted. He didn't recognize the voice. Was Challies with them? Or had he fled as well? A new surge of panic hit Rex with the realization that the Ætherian Council and the ACF would know that Challies had helped him. Would he be Tossed?

"There!" The scream tore Rex from his thoughts.

And without hesitating further, he swiped Challies's Nanokepp Card over the Zipp line's magnetic card reader and pushed Aral to the edge of the platform. Just before she fell over the edge, he jumped up across Aral's stomach, wedging his legs around her waist. He squeezed as tight as his fatigued muscles would allow and latched his frozen feet together behind her back. He wrapped his good arm around her shoulders in a hug of life and dug his fingers into her arm.

With a scrape, the two leaned over the precipice and Zipped out over the void, the ACF closing in upon them, Stær guns drawn.

FOURTEEN

ARAL AND REX COLLIDED INTO ISLAND Twenty-Three just as the one hundred thousand-volt Stær volley launched over the chasm after them.

Fortunately, they were out of range.

Behind them, the Stær sparks popped in the moonlit night, not hitting their target. Whipping away instantly in the seventy-mile-per-hour wind, they formed streaking lines of orange and yellow across the sky. Rex didn't pause to admire the fireworks. As soon as their frostbitten feet hit the surface of Island Twenty-Four, he fumbled with Aral's harness to release her. The two tumbled to the ground in a clump. Rex screamed at the pain in his shoulder.

"Feet . . . " Aral muttered.

"I know, I know. Me too," he chattered. His cheeks and ears burned from the cold, and his eyes stung from the wind. Because he'd been using his left hand to grip Aral and it had been against her body, he retained movement and feeling in his one usable hand. With the shouts of the ACF troops growing closer, he moved quickly, pulling himself up on his knees.

"C'mon!" he snapped, standing and pulling at Aral's arm. "We're almost there! There are masks in there! I've got the key!"

In reply, Aral groaned and made a feeble attempt to stand. Gritting his teeth against the pain, Rex pulled her up and the two shuffled the twenty yards from the island's edge to the hangar entrance. Rex stopped in front of the door's magnetic key sensor.

Fumbling with Challies's Nanokepp Card, Rex turned and looked behind him. The ACF troops had harnessed in and were beginning to slide over the expanse. Aral saw them too. They were still faint enough that, to the ACF, Rex and Aral's silhouettes probably melted into the dark mass of the building. With any luck, they'd think Rex and Aral had run around the building to try and escape over another Zipp line. After all, how could they know that Rex had Challies's Nanokepp Card?

"There they are!" Aral screamed into Rex's ear in the clearest voice since she'd spoken in the Sanatorium room.

"I know, I know . . . " Rex answered as he slid Challies's card over the sensor. The sensor flashed green and emitted a soft *beep-beep*. The warehouse door clicked open.

Supporting Aral with his good arm, Rex kicked the door in and pulled the two inside. As he did, his left side slammed into what must've been a barrel filled with metal rods that someone had placed near the door. With an ear-splitting crash, the container upended, sending the rods sprawling over the concrete floor. Metallic clangs, clanks, crashes, and bangs echoed through the dark storeroom. Rex groaned at the noise, which the ACF troops could surely hear over the wailing wind. *Oh no,* Rex thought. *They'll know we went inside . . .*

He slammed the door shut behind him with a metallic thud. The automatic bolt re-engaged, locking them inside.

But the ACF would soon be there.

And they would have their own Nanokepp Cards.

Rex looked around. The last time he was here he'd been with Schlott and his entire Unit Alif, just before they made their first descent into Cthonia. Then, the warehouse and its hundreds of stocked shelves had been well-lit. But now, in the middle of the night, when most of Ætheria was sleeping, only the soft blue luminescent glow from the security lights gave the two a sickly, bluish pallor.

Rex blinked to allow his eyes to adjust to the dim glow, as they still smarted from the flash of the Stær sparks. He tried to orient himself. To either side of the room, he discerned the towering shelves he'd seen before, containing all manner of pipes, stratoneum, nuts, bolts, and hardware necessary to keep Ætheria up and running . . . or to rebuild a destroyed Power Works and Proboscis.

"Hang on," he said, lowering Aral to the floor next to the door. She crumpled into a slack seated position, her head down. Rex stepped over to the pile of metal scrap he'd upended and knelt, feeling through the pieces with frozen fingers. The metal clanged against the floor as he pushed rods and slivers out of the way. Finding what he was looking for, Rex clamped his hand over two small pieces. Rods, each about a foot long, tapered into a wedge. He turned back to the door and jammed the pointed ends in between the door and its frame. With a thud, they stuck. But Rex bent back down to the pile and felt around until he found a larger, heavier piece. With his improvised tool in hand, he swirled back to the door and pounded on the rods, wedging them further into place.

BAM! BAM! BAM! The din of the metal-on-metal

was deafening, and the sound resonated throughout the building like a massive drum. The vibration and jolt of the impact sent jolts up Rex's only good arm and to his wounded shoulder. Tears sprang to his eyes as he tried to focus on what he had to do and not let the pain overwhelm him.

Rex tossed his makeshift mallet and reached down for Aral. He grabbed her arm and pulled. She moaned. Her head lolled almost unconsciously from shoulder to shoulder.

"Come on . . . " he said, pulling with all his strength. Aral's legs stirred awake and she struggled to her feet. Rex pulled her arm once more around his shoulder and turned to the middle of the warehouse.

He took a few steps forward. About ten yards in front of him, he could just make out the ghostly forms of the descent pods lying in a row like a dozen coffins, their hatches open. By now, he hoped, the warehouse personnel had had time to restock them with full oxygen canisters.

He hoped.

"There," Rex said, more to himself than to Aral. He shuffled over to the farthest descent pod and rotated Aral around his body and onto the padded seat. He knew that this pod would be the first down, as it was closest to the trap door . . . just like before. Aral groaned as she lay flat, resting her head on the headrest. With his eyes now adjusting to the gloom, Rex reached in and felt around the interior of the pod, squinting at each cranny of the device. When he'd made his descent, Yoné had attached his SCRM to an oxygen tank in a small compartment to the left of the passenger. His fingers, only just beginning to thaw from the frigid night air, latched onto a hook. He pulled and a small door popped open. He reached his hand in and closed it around a cold, circular cylinder. They had restocked the oxygen!

"That's it!" he shouted, making Aral jump in her weakened state. Half-squinting, half-feeling his way through the dark, he pulled the tank out and laid it on Aral's chest.

"Here," he said, pulling her weakened arms up and

over the tank to hold it in place. He glanced franti-
cally around the warehouse but knew he wouldn't see
what he was looking for.

"I don't know where they keep the masks, or if
there are any here," he stammered. "So you need to
hold this up close to your mouth. Try to breathe in
the air . . ."

With that, he reached to the top of the canister
and turned the knob clockwise as far as it would go.
There was an audible hiss, and he felt Aral's hair puff
out and away from her face. The oxygen was flow-
ing. Satisfied that he could turn the knob no more,
he began using his good hand to strap Aral in. Aral
scrunched up her nose like someone about to sneeze,
but then leaned her head forward and toward the
streaming air.

"I'm sorry," he said, pulling gently at her head to
help her get close to the tank. "It's almost over."

"It's working," Aral mumbled as Rex worked
the straps over her shoulders. Her voice, weakened

from the lack of oxygen, startled him. "I'm feeling better . . ."

"Good," Rex said. Relief flooded him. But rather than let the emotion paralyze him in a moment of sentimentality, he worked even faster.

BOOM! BOOM! BOOM!

Someone pounded at the door.

The ACF.

"Open up in there! You're not in trouble! We just need to talk to you!" shouted a muffled voice from outside. Rex thought he recognized Roman's voice, but he wasn't sure. He shot a glance at the door. *No way,* he thought. He was certain that getting caught— or even turning himself in—would be disastrous . . . if not for him, then definitely for Aral. And Challies had already warned him about the danger of being Tossed. And now? Now that he'd help Aral escape?

BOOM! BOOM! BOOM! came the pounding again, filling the building with the dull, metallic thud of angry fists.

"Listen," Rex said, looking around. His eyes

quickly found what they were looking for. "On the wall is the release button. I've done this before—but last time I was in one of these. I'm going to close the hatch and press the button, and you'll head back down through a trap door. Like the one we went through when we came up."

"Trap door? What trap door?" Aral tried to sit up and look around, the whistling oxygen tank slipping across her chest. Rex noticed that her voice was beginning to sound clearer, healthier. Though it would be better concentrated inside a SCRM, the oxygen was working.

"I'll follow you," he said. "Don't worry."

Nodding, Aral leaned back and laid her head on the rest. Rex reached up and pulled the pod's hatch shut. It latched in place.

BOOM! BOOM!

"We're warning you! In the name of the Head Ductor and the Ætherian High Command, unblock this door . . . NOW!"

With Aral safely inside the descent pod, Rex

stepped back to the wall and lifted a hinged, clear plastic box from the wall, where it protected a large blue button. Without hesitating, he punched the button. A short, high-pitched bell rang in acknowledgement, and in the next second, the floor to the foot of Aral's descent pod opened up.

The faint, bluish-reddish light of dawn burst into the room, filling the compartment with a much warmer glow . . . one that allowed Rex to see the descent pods clearly. He had the impression that they were shinier than the last time he'd taken one, as if someone had polished them for their next use.

The trap doors swung downward. Light poured in from below, lighting Aral's pod at a strange angle and making it seem as if the pod itself were glowing.

With the trap doors fully open, the coffin-like vehicle lurched into motion and vanished downward.

Rex released the button and the trap door closed.

BOOM! BOOM! BOOM! CRUNCH! CRA-CRACK!

The door was breaking open.

Just before Rex stepped over to his pod, a new fear struck. The trap doors were designed to be opened by at least two people—one latched in for descent and the other at the button. He remembered his trainer mentioning to him that this design had been created "to avoid accidents." Rex cursed at himself and cast his eyes around the room. An idea struck. A bad idea, but the only one that presented itself.

CRAAAAACK!

In a panic, he stepped back over to the plastic protector box and lifted it clear of the blue button, which protruded about two inches from the wall. With the box clear of the button, he pushed it to the top of its hinge range and let go. As the box began to fall back into place he yanked his fist back and punched. His blow hit hard on the side of the box, cracking one of the plastic hinges. He pulled back and punched two more times. And on the third punch, the entire cover snapped off and tumbled to the floor with a broken rattle. He rushed back over to the shelves and filled his arms with tools: hammers, wrenches, extra winch sets, and two extra SCRM oxygen tanks. He shuffled back to his own pod and kneeled in the passenger compartment. He let the tools tumble around him in a pile.

With arm trembling, he picked up the hammer, took aim, and threw the tool at the blue button, which sat mocking him from the wall. Even though he was left-handed and now using his dominant hand, having his knees penned in by the descent pod caused him to flail about clumsily. And when he threw, his wounded shoulder ripped in pain, causing his aim to waver and him to send the hammer hurtling off nearly a yard from its intended target.

"No . . . " he muttered, picking up the wrench and throwing. He missed. He threw one of the masks. Missed.

CRAAAACK!

Hearing the most violent crack since the ACF troops began pounding, Rex jerked his head in the direction of the door. And to his horror, he saw early-morning daylight flooding into the warehouse, followed by the menacing shadows of the troops as they teemed in, their Staer guns drawn. At first he was surprised—and slightly relieved—that none of them carried lights. This meant they probably couldn't see him right away. *But surely they heard the bell as Aral went down? Surely they knew what Rex and Aral were doing . . .*

His heart pounding and his hands covered in sweat, Rex turned his attention back to the blue release button. He picked up one of the oxygen containers. He tried to steady his breath and his shaking hand. He took aim. He threw. He missed.

At the clang of the oxygen canister smacking against the wall and tumbling to the floor, the ACF troops turned in unison in Rex's direction.

"There!" someone shouted. "At the pod! I see him!"

"Don't move!" another voice shouted. Rex thought he recognized Roman's voice. He sounded furious.

Gritting his teeth and fighting back panic, Rex

picked up the one remaining oxygen canister and reared his left arm back.

"Give up now, or we'll fire!"

Rex held his breath. Keeping his eyes fixed on the release button, he gripped the oxygen canister, aimed, and hurled the device as hard as he could. "Aaaahhh!" he screamed, as the momentum of his throw cause his wounded shoulder to smack into the descent pod's open hatch door. Pain shot through his body.

Just inside the warehouse door, Roman began to squeeze the trigger to his Stær gun.

The oxygen tank flew through the air, covering the short ten feet between Rex and the button. Rex jerked his hand down and grabbed the shoulder straps inside the descent pod. The oxygen tank clanged at it struck its target. It was a direct hit. The warning bell sounded. The sound startled Roman, who squeezed his trigger all the way. The Stær gun beeped and fired, sending out charges of one hundred thousand volts of electricity. The trap doors swung open with a hiss. The outside air rushed in with a blast of frigid air.

The daylight stung Rex's eyes. Roman also squinted, his eyes smarting. He didn't see if his shot had struck Rex.

Because in the next millisecond, Rex Himmel, fugitive of the state of Ætheria, had vanished below in a stolen descent pod.

FIFTEEN

THE ACF WAS IN CRISIS MODE. NO SOONER HAD Aral and Rex disappeared below in the descent pods than Roman had radioed in the news of the unprecedented breakout. And within minutes, the rumor shot through the entire twenty-four-island archipelago that someone had helped them. Someone on the inside. A traitor.

Challies.

"After them! What are you waiting for?!" The ten scouts shouted as Rex's pod slipped through the trap door and out of sight. By the time he had vanished, Aral's pod was already several hundred yards down the guy wire, approaching the toxic Welcans cloud that separated Ætheria from Cthonia.

"Let's go!"

"Get into the pods!"

"They're only a few seconds ahead of us!"

"Come on! We can catch them!"

"Wait, wait!" Roman shouted over the others. At his order, the other nine wavered, their nervous hands toying with their pulsing Stær guns. In this state of agitation, the slightest surprise might cause them to fire. Their every nerve was on edge.

"What is it?" one of the scouts asked, his lip trembling from the adrenaline coursing through his body.

"Hold on!" Roman raised one hand, showing his palm for the scouts to stand down. He gripped his Stær gun in his right hand. "We don't have clearance . . . not yet—not to go down. I have to check with Bernuac HQ."

The soldiers exchanged nervous glances, their trigger fingers hovering anxiously aside their guns. Their breath came in short, labored gasps. They were like sharks who'd tasted blood and were ready for the kill. Despite the freezing temperatures of Ætheria's thirty thousand foot altitude, their foreheads shone with sweat. Roman fumbled with a small receiver clipped onto his shoulder strap.

"HQ, this is Protector Roman 3366."

"Yes, we hear you, Roman. Status on the fugitive?" A burst of static punctuated the transmitter's sentences.

"Yes, there are two fugitives: the boy Rex Himmel and the Cthonian who was in custody at the Sanatorium. They've escaped from the Sanatorium. They're gone."

"Gone?! Where are they now?"

"They've fled down the descent pods to Cthonia. I believe they went in two pods. Yes, two pods are missing."

"Sorry, Roman, we didn't get that. Can you repeat? You say they have succeeded in getting out of Ætheria? Escaping? What?! And down the descent pods? Come again."

"I repeat: the two fugitives, Rex Himmel and the Cthonian infiltrator, have somehow broken out of the Sanatorium and have gone down toward the Welcans cloud in two separate descent pods. I am requesting permission to give pursuit immediately. We might still catch them if we hurry."

A pause filled the strained silence in the Island Twenty-Four warehouse, where the descent pods and trap doors were located. It was here that the ACF had to come to inspect the support strut anchors supporting the floating islands down below. Every two months, an inspection team went down to the Cthonian wasteland to check on the foundations and supports for any signs of wear or corrosion. For regular maintenance of the wires or struts themselves, the ACF could use harnesses and descend from individual islands by winch, via the Larders. In addition to emergency supply stores, the Larders contained guy wire anchors for lines that descended all the way to Cthonia. But throughout Ætheria's history, the past few weeks were the only time anyone ever took the Island Twenty-Four descent pods down for any other reason than routine maintenance. And this was to send down a team of scouts to investigate the Cthonian attack on Ætheria. Now, Roman awaited permission to send down another unit of the Ætherian Cover Force. But armed.

"Sorry, Roman 3366, permission denied. We don't have clearance from the Head Ductor. There are other, bigger plans in place; and we need everyone here. The HD will brief everyone soon. Besides, do you even have SCRMs? You'd be dead the moment you stepped out and onto land below."

With a strained expression, Roman darted his eyes around the warehouse for extra SCRMs—Self-Contained Respiratory Masks—that would allow him to breathe on the inhospitable Cthonian surface. He scanned the hundreds of shelves piled high with every sort of replacement mechanical piece necessary to keep Ætheria running and habitable. He knew that the pods usually contained their own oxygen canisters, but passengers had to hook up their own masks. As he looked around, he recalled Rex's dogged insistence that the air down below was actually better than the air in Ætheria. Roman shook his head. What sort of idiots did Rex think the ACF were? What kind of trap was he trying to set? And to think: Rex had actually been *recruited* into the ACF because the Head Ductor had wanted it! Roman had always had his doubts about that kid. And now there was no way he was about to let some little punk's lies get him killed from asphyxiation.

"I don't see any masks here. I repeat: there are no masks," Roman spat into his receiver. The static snapped as he released the transmit button. "But aren't they locked up here? Or on a shelf somewhere? If you could just tell me where they are stored, we could . . . "

Roman's voice died off as his thoughts took control. Silence filled the room. Roman could hear his own heartbeat over his scouts' panting, which was gradually slowing.

No one answered his transmission. *What was going*

on? Roman looked at his receiver and shook it, as if trying to shake parts of it loose.

"Bernuac HQ, can anyone hear me? Hello? We are losing time!"

Roman looked around at his scouts. Their eyes were trained on him, awaiting his orders.

"Roman 3366, are you there? Can you hear me?"

"Roman here, what next?"

"Is Challies 2496 with you? Over."

"Challies? No." Roman looked around. His men followed his lead, glancing around the warehouse as if expecting Challies to appear. "I haven't seen him since we were dismissed yesterday evening, after admitting the prisoner to the Sanatorium. But I think . . . "

"What is it?"

"I'm sure he dazed me back in the Sanatorium when I was guarding the boy Rex Himmel. It had to have been him."

"Why do you think that?"

"I was standing there one second, and the next I woke up in the boy's room. And he was gone. Challies didn't answer my radio calls, and when I went to the Cthonian's room, Challies was gone. None of the nurses had seen anything. I don't see what else it could've been. And he has been acting strange lately . . . "

"Roman, we understand. Right now, you need to call off your scouts immediately and report to Bernuac HQ. We've just received other intelligence, and we need to act."

Roman shook his head and furrowed his brow.

"What? Abandon the chase?! Give up? We have two fugitives and are in pursuit. If we can just get clearance and masks, we can go and—"

"I said *no*, Roman!" The voice on the other end was testy. "You will do as you're told. We have bigger problems than your two prisoners, and we need all ACF at Bernuac immediately for a situation report and orders. Get over here *now*."

"Problem? What problem?"

"Challies has disappeared. *Gone*. We found his Tracker on the southeast side of the Sanatorium.

Removed. He'd cut it off somehow, and . . . " the voice trailed off amid static.

"Yes? Go ahead, HQ. Your signal broke up. What was that?"

"I said, without someone's help, there's no way that kid and that Cthonian could've escaped. Protector Challies had to have helped them, and now he's on the run. We've got to find him before he does something else. Maybe he's even gone down below?"

"But the fugitives? They're getting away! And only two pods are missing here. He must still be in Ætheria . . . "

"I'm telling you, the Head Ductor has something planned—something far bigger than just finding Challies or catching those two criminals. We will catch them, but not with just a few ACF."

"What are we going to do?"

"We're going to take down an army."